I0600468

Camille

A new version of Alexandre Dumas's
La Dame au Camelias

by Pam Gems

A SAMUEL FRENCH ACTING EDITION

SAMUEL FRENCH

FOUNDED 1830

New York Hollywood London Toronto

SAMUELFRENCH.COM

Camille was first presented at The Other Place, Stratford-upon-Avon, by the Royal Shakespeare Company on 4 April 1984. It was directed by Ron Daniels; Maria Bjornson was the designer and the lighting was by John Waterhouse. Guy Woolfenden arranged the music, choreography was by Anthony van Laast, fights arranged by Malcolm Ransom. Richard Oriel was the stage manager.

The cast was as follows:

MARGUERITE GAUTIER	Frances Barber
ARMAND DUVAL	Nicholas Farrell
PRUDENCE DE MARSAN DE TALBEC	Polly James
SOPHIE DE LYONNE	Alphonsia Emmanuel
CLÉMENCE DE VILLENEUVE	Rowena Roberts
JANINE/OLYMPE	Katharine Rogers
YVETTE	Sarah Woodward
GASTON DE MAURIEUX	Paul Gregory
LE DUC	Norman Henry
COUNT DRUFTHEIM	Charles Millham
M. DE SANCERRE	Arthur Kohn
PRINCE BELA MIRKASSIAN	Andrew Hall
JEAN	Peter Theedom
UPHOLSTERER	Andrew Jarvis
JEAN-PAUL	Brian McGinley or Richard Parry
GRAVEDIGGER	Peter Theedom
INSPECTOR	Norman Henry
PIERRE	Andrew Jarvis
ARMAND'S FATHER, THE MARQUIS DE SAINT-BRIEUC	Bernard Horsfall
RUSSIAN PRINCE (SERGEI)	Arthur Kohn

Other parts were played by members of the company. The pianist was James Walker.

LONG WHARF THEATRE

Presents
the American Premiere

CAMILLE
BY PAM GEMS

Directed by
RON DANIELS

Scenery by
MING CHO LEE

Costumes by
JESS GOLDSTEIN

Lighting by
RONALD WALLACE

Music Consultant
TERRENCE SHERMAN

Dance and movement by
WESLEY FATA

Wigs and hairstyles by
PAUL HUNTLEY

Production Stage Manager
BEVERLY J. ANDREOZZI

November 29, 1986 – January 11, 1987

Arvin Brown, Artistic Director
M. Edgar Rosenblum, Executive Director

THE CAST   (in order of appearance)

Armand Duval	**RAMY ZADA**
Prudence de Maison de Talbec	**SASHA VON SCHOELER**
Clemence de Villeneuve	**KIT LEFEVER**
Sophie de Lyonne	**JANET HUBERT**
Monsieur le Duc	**WILLIAM SWETLAND**
Count Druftheim	**DAVID PIERCE**
Marguerite Gautier	**KATHLEEN TURNER**
Monsieur de Sancerre	**DAVID JAFFE**
Janine/Olympe	**GINA GERSHON**
Pierre	**JONO GERO**
Jean-Paul	**BRENDAN BLOOM**
	MARK GENTILE
Yvette	**CHRISTIE MCGINN**
Marquis de Saint-Brieux	**REX ROBBINS**
The Russian Prince	**DAVID JAFFE**
The Appraiser	**JONO GERO**
Footmen	**DAVID SHIMCHICK**
	NICK SANDYS
Pianist	**JAMES GEMMELL**

Paris, in the late 1840's.

The action takes place in the Foyer Cafe of the Paris Opera House, at the apartments of Marguerite Gautier and Armand Duval and in the garden of a country house several miles south of Paris.

THERE WILL BE ONE INTERMISSION

THE CAST

MARGUERITE GAUTIER
ARMAND DUVAL
PRUDENCE DE MAISON DE TALBEC
CLEMENCE DE VILLENEUVE
SOPHIE DE LYONNE
MONSIEUR LE DUC
COUNT DRUFTHEIM
GASTON DE MAURIEUX
HONORE DE SANCERRE
JANINE/OLYMPE DE POITIERS
PIERRE
JEAN-PAUL
YVETTE
THE MARQUIS DE SAINT-BRIEUC
THE RUSSIAN PRINCE
THE BAILIFF
TWO GRAVEDIGGERS
THE INSPECTOR
TWO FOOTMEN
PIANIST

NOTES ON CHARACTERS

MARGUERITE is characterised by a gentleness and a sweetness that seem at odds with her metier as a successful Parisian courtesan . . . perhaps it is the secret of her success. Certainly she has a hot temper, when we see the peasant girl, but her rages are without spite, and her temperament is generous to a fault. She has a fine sense of humour and the ridiculous. On the dark side she has frightening dips into a deathly depression, when she seems, often momentarily, a deathly shadow of herself. And she can founder in hysteria, as when she is threatened with the removal of her child. Then we see her lose control. In her attraction to, and then her growing love for Armand we see her at first gently genial, then troubled and challenged. There is a great deal of the maternal in her love for him. She loves him, as distinct from being attracted to him physically, when he talks of his loveless childhood. She sees that he, too, has suffered deprivation.

ARMAND appears to be shining flower of the aristocracy, well-dressed, perfectly mannered. But under the geniality a devil pops out from time to time, there is blackness, he plays jokes that are not entirely benevolent. ARMAND is like KAY in The Snow Queen. He has ice in his heart. Brought up as an aristocrat, he has been reared by servants. Thus his personal relationships, relationships of affection, have also been power relationships . . . his nanny has been his servant. He has seen little of his own parents, they lead prescribed social lives. ARMAND, rich and powerful, can buy all the affection he needs. And despises the sellers. His life, it seems, is mapped out for him from cradle to grave.

PRUDENCE was a courtesan. Now, older, she maintains a tolerable standard of living by acting as a discreet go-between. She is a shrewd survivor. She sees both sides.

SOPHIE is a Bohemian. A white-faced girl with frizzed hair and a large velvet bonnet, she is one of the new breed of independant women. She will go where she pleases, with whom she pleases. She consorts with artists, frequents the Latin quarter. She will accept introductions from Prudence when it suits her (or when she needs the money badly). But SOPHIE cherishes her independance, and is prepared to accept the concomitant risks in her life.

CLEMENCE is of a different temperament. CLEMENCE likes to be comfortable. She likes eating, she likes presents, pretty things like kittens. She likes pleasing, and making people comfortable. She is, in fact, a conjugal girl. Thus, for CLEMENCE, happiness is to be found in the security of a good marriage. She is prepared to give as much as she gets, to give comfort, attention, to nurse, be a good listener, wait at home, admire, console. For that she will be showered with gifts and attention and affection. She is not a brilliant girl . . . arithmetic at school will have been a trial . . . but she has a native shrewdness. She finds her moments, picks the chances that come her way. She prattles, this she finds eases the moments, makes people feel relaxed. She does not play the clown, she is a successful courtesan in her own right and doesn't need to beg for favour. But she likes a light and happy atmosphere; and she helps it along.

JANINE/OLYMPE JANINE is on the way up. Several years younger than the other girls, she apes them, and seeks to be one of them. She lacks social graces, but is a good mimic, and never misses a chance to assert herself, to draw the men's attention to herself. She is ambitious, and cold, though she has a lot of shining vivacity.

She is not in the least in love with Armand, though she has a certain detached respect for his viciousness. The acme of her desire is to be the maitresse en titre of the old Duke.

COUNT DRUFTHEIM, from Sweden. He is, as we see, very shy. He is travelling and seeing the world. He is a booby in some ways, a provincial. But we do see the provincial virtues . . . his sweetness of temper, his kindness . . . his genuine love of music, of the arts . . . his enthusiastic amazement at the phenomena of life. He alone shows an interest in anything other than the milieu.

THE FATHER. The only time we see the MARQUIS DE BRIEUC is when there is urgent business to perform. We do not see him visit his son for any other reason. His manner is almost always urbane. His power is such that he has rarely found it necessary to raise his voice. So he has trouble containing rage. But his training, life, and the necessity to remove Marguerite G. from his path for the sake of his title, estate and family, mean that he uses all the weapons that are necessary, both direct and indirect . . . both a clubman bonhomie to Armand, and the use of blackmail to Marguerite. If he seems cruel, one must remember the stakes, and the threat to his family.

NOTE: The period of the play is 1848. The dresses, therefore, are bell-shaped rather than the full crinolines of the 1860s, and the women's hair is dressed with ringlets, giving a gentle, fragile and flowerlike appearance.

Camille

ACT ONE

*Scene One — A room in the house of Marguerite Gautier.
The furniture is covered with dustsheets, and labels
are attached to the legs of chairs.*

AUCTIONEER. (*off*) Lot one hundred and twenty
four . . . one steel fender, fire irons en suite, ditto
firedogs — may I have your bids for this handsome lot,
please? Fifty francs? Fifty francs, Monsieur. Fifty-
five . . . sixty — hold them up, boy — there, fit for a
gentleman's residence . . . I'm bid sixty . . . yes sir,
sixty-five? Can I see seventy? Seventy, Milord — a mod-
est memento to be sure — and seventy-five —

(*A young man enters abruptly, brushing past a man on
the door who closes the door after him, cutting off the
sound. The young man looks pale, dazed, perhaps he is
ill. He looks about the room, then begins to recognize
pieces of furniture. He touches them, becoming agitated
and aware. The man at the door, for a tip, allows another
man to enter. He is older, heavier. He strolls, curious.
The first man becomes aware of him.*)

ARMAND. Who are you, what do you want?
GASTON. Sir?
ARMAND. What are you doing?
GASTON. I beg your pardon. I simply came to see.
ARMAND. See? See what?
GASTON. Forgive me, it seems that I am intruding. I

was enjoying the spring sunshine . . . a shower drove me in, the crowd intrigued me. I beg your pardon.(*He makes to go but ARMAND groans softly.*) My dear sir, you're ill!

ARMAND. It's nothing. A fever. I was in Egypt.

GASTON. Ah indeed. I am well acquainted with the rigours of foreign infection — I have been travelling myself. (*He picks up an ornament, but, at ARMAND's glance, puts it down again.*) Persia . . . the Levant, for over a year. (*slight pause*) I lost my dear wife.

ARMAND. Lost?

GASTON. In childbirth.

AUCTIONEER. (*Off*) Chere Madame, don't resist! (*laughter, off*) Fifteen bonnets, all trimmed? (*laughter, off*)

ARMAND. And the child? Her child?

GASTON. In the coffin with his mother.

AUCTIONEER. (*bangs gavel*) Thank you! Sold to the enchanting Mam'selle by the window. Adieu the bonnets, or may we hope au revoir? (*laughter.*)

GASTON. (*closing the door*) You are not here to buy?

ARMAND. Buy?

GASTON. A remembrance perhaps? The house is full of the most lovely things . . . alas, all going for a price. (*His statement seems to arouse ARMAND, who rises abruptly and listens at the door as the auctioneer speaks.*)

AUCTIONEER. Lot one hundred and thirty, a fine looking glass, silver gilt is described — five hundred francs . . . thank you, sir — six hundred . . . seven . . . and eight . . . one thousand. One thousand francs, ladies and gentlemen, for this fine mirror. Going at —

ARMAND. (*calls*) Two thousand.

GASTON. Oh but —

AUCTIONEER. Two thousand behind me. And one? And one. And two. And three. And four?

ARMAND. Three thousand. (*A murmur, off. GASTON raises a hand, shrugs.*)

AUCTIONEER. Three thousand. And two fifty. Three thousand five . . . seven-fifty — thank you, sir, and —

ARMAND. Five thousand! (*A gasp from the crowd, off.*)

GASTON. No, enough!

AUCTIONEER. (*Quickly*) Five thousand . . . five thousand for this fine mirror . . . (*Bangs gavel*) . . . sold to the gentleman behind me! And now, Mesdames et Messieur the lot you've all been waiting for. The last lot, ladies and gentlemen. The bed. As sketched in the journals, you've all read about it . . . decorated with — what are they, boy?

BOY. (*Offstage*) Camellias, sir!

AUCTIONEER. To be sure. Camellias. What was it? Twenty-three days of the month she wore white camellias . . . the other five days she wore red . . . (*laughter.*)

ARMAND. (*Low*) No . . .

AUCTIONEER. Truth of it, sir. There it is, ladies and gentlemen, the bed . . . as shown — a unique piece of carving . . . quite lovely . . . cherubs, swans, and the . . . ah . . . the ah . . . camellias . . . pointe de Venise trimmed sheets and pillows extant still — don't push, please. What am I bid? For this beautiful bed? (*Silence.*) I shall want a good price. (*Silence.*)

ARMAND. No.

AUCTIONEER. You bidding, sir?

GASTON. I think the gentleman is ill.

VOICE. Two hundred thousand for the bed!

VOICE2. And fifty!

VOICE. Three hundred thousand —

AUCTIONEER. Thank you, sirs — three hundred thousand I'm bid, three hundred thousand —

ARMAND. No! No! No! (*GASTON pulls him away from the door, pushes him onto a chair. The sound of the gavel arouses ARMAND as from a dream.*)

GASTON. You are too late, my friend. The bed is sold, the auction is over. (*Gently*) You knew the lady. (*Slight pause.*) May I know her name? (*But ARMAND seems in a dream.*) May I know the lady's name? (*ARMAND looks up at him, dazed, and then rises urgently and rushes out. GASTON, astonished, pauses, then, alarmed, makes after him swiftly.*)

SCENE TWO

The foyer of the Paris Opera House. Enter Prudence, Clemence and Sophie, and, separately, two waiters. The women circulate, using their fans, curtseying to the old duke as he enters.

DUKE. Ah, hahaha . . . the three Graces, eh? (*Pinches PRUDENCE.*) Fat as ever, eh, Prudence? . . . fat as ever!

PRUDENCE. (*Putting on a high social style for him*) Dear Duke! . . . such wit, always the wit!

DUKE. Pretty fine looking woman that soprano — heh? (*Nudges her suggestively. PRUDENCE smiles sweetly.*) What do you think of her execution?

PRUDENCE. (*Sweet*) Oh I'm all for it, Duke, I'm all for it — (*Aside, to SOPHIE —*) thank God for intermissions.

CLEMENCE. You aren't enjoying the opera? You mean it? I'm Very affected!

SOPHIE. That's true.

CLEMENCE. Oh Sophie, you're so hard — what's wrong with being moved?

PRUDENCE. By a three hundred pound elephant? Not my idea of a prima donna . . . apart from the singing . . .

SOPHIE. Not to mention the baritone's crossed eyes —

PRUDENCE. And we all know why that is — never mind, dear, it's medical.

CLEMENCE. I don't care what you say, I believe in it all!

PRUDENCE. That will get you nowhere.

CLEMENCE. I don't see why not. Anything's possible.

SOPHIE. You believe in fairy tales?

CLEMENCE. Why not? After all, we're all inventions —(*PRUDENCE clears her throat, jerks her head slightly CLEMENCE obediently accosts the young Count Druftheim.*) Good-evening. We met in Ostend, don't you remember — or was it Baden-Baden?

COUNT. (*Stiff*) Excuse me please, I am in the opera losing my hat. (*Escapes.*)

PRUDENCE. His hat! Poor boy.

SOPHIE. Yes. Serious matter.

CLEMENCE. What, losing your hat? (*Sees that they are teasing.*) Well, I like him, I'm good with shy men.

SOPHIE. I fancy he's already taken.

CLEMENCE. Oh, who by? Armand! (*ARMAND is standing in the door.*)

PRUDENCE. Oh there you are. Well?

CLEMENCE. You're wicked. (*She pouts.*) Well? Did you win?

ARMAND. (*Bows.*) Seven. On the black.

PRUDENCE. You don't mean it? Seven in a row?

SOPHIE. At the table?

PRUDENCE. The odds!

CLEMENCE. Aren't you clever, isn't he clever?

PRUDENCE. Waiter, champagne — we must celebrate! I'll arrange a party, an orchestra — what is it, what's the matter?

SOPHIE. (*Laughs*) Could it be that the eighth throw was red?

ARMAND. (*Bows, laughing*) Apologies. From the heart.

PRUDENCE. You never know when to leave off. Carry on like this, you'll ruin yourself, and you can stop that — (*As ARMAND kisses CLEMENCE's hand gallantly —*) she wants nothing more to do with you, you've broken that poor girl's heart —

ARMAND. La Belle Clemence —

PRUDENCE. — she hasn't forgiven you, have you?

CLEMENCE. What? (*Obedient*) No.

PRUDENCE. I had to prise the laudanum from her poor little hand, she was going to finish it all — weren't you?

CLEMENCE. What? Yes.

PRUDENCE. She'd even chosen the hymns for her funeral —

CLEMENCE. (*Dreamy*) I'm having masses of white violets — and tuberoses, for the smell . . .

PRUDENCE. And her body's to be shipped to Lisbon.

SOPHIE. Why Lisbon?

CLEMENCE. Because I've never been there, silly.

ARMAND. (*To SOPHIE, with a bow*) Mamselle de Lyonne?

SOPHIE. Monsieur Duval?

ARMAND. I thought we'd seen the last of you.

SOPHIE. You seem surprised.

ARMAND. By you?

PRUDENCE. Armand, that's enough.

ARMAND. Where have you been?

SOPHIE. Where? At the opera.

ARMAND. No doubt an — elevating — experience?

SOPHIE. Alas, the bass was disappointing.

ARMAND. Oh, in what way?

SOPHIE. A trifle insufficient. (*She smiles up at him coolly and turns away. Snubbed, he turns to CLEMENCE, lifts her gently but firmly by the elbow.*)

CLEMENCE. Armand, no . . .

PRUDENCE. She'll miss the last act — (*But ARMAND and CLEMENCE go. Short pause.*) Where DID you go?

SOPHIE. To Dieppe.

PRUDENCE. Hmmm . . . a long way to buy a crochet hook, if I may say so. *I* could have helped you.

SOPHIE. (*Dry*) Yes.

PRUDENCE. My dear, you're a fool to fall out with Armand. Fine family, well in funds —

SOPHIE. No.

PRUDENCE. Why not? You still interest him. Have patience, I've been his friend for a long time —

SOPHIE. Then you know him. (*They exchange a glance.*)

PRUDENCE. He's a dear boy, I won't hear a word against him, your trouble is you're too independant —

SOPHIE. (*Kisses her cheek then she turns, amused, as CLEMENCE enters, followed by ARMAND.*) Ah . . . the lovers! Back again . . . so soon?

(*ARMAND looks at her briefly, crosses and stands behind PRUDENCE. He looks down at her with a strange, blank expression. She looks up at him, shakes her head slightly. He bends, begins to stroke her bare arm gently.*)

PRUDENCE. (*Purrs*) Armand . . . you're a wicked boy. Why can't you treat us decently?

ARMAND. (*To himself*) What is it with women's arms? There's something honest about them — (*She smiles as he bends to kiss her arm. But then he bites, making her scream with pain.*)

PRUDENCE. Stop it, you brute!

ARMAND. Ah, Prudence . . . your flesh, so white, so mature . . .

PRUDENCE. You're too rough!

ARMAND. But worth your while.

PRUDENCE. The pawnbroker doesn't think so. (*She makes to go, he follows.*)

PRUDENCE. Armand, why must you be so cruel?

ARMAND. Cruel?

PRUDENCE. With women. Why?

ARMAND. They disappoint.

(*He looks up as MARGUERITE GAUTIER appears, followed by an older man. ARMAND sees MAR- GUERITE. MARGUERITE sees ARMAND. There is a prolonged, still pause as they regard each other.*)

ARMAND. Who is that?

PRUDENCE. Marguerite. Come away, she's not for you.

ARMAND. Why not?

PRUDENCE. For one thing, you couldn't afford her.

ARMAND. Why not?

PRUDENCE. My dear, no-one can!

MARGUERITE. (*At a distance*) Who is that?

DE SANCERRE. Armand Duval. The son of the Mar- quis de Brieuc.

MARGUERITE. (*Looks briefly past DE SANCERRE to*

ARMAND) Will you forgive me if I talk to some friends? (*He bows coldly, turns away.*) Shall I see you later tonight?

DE SANCERRE. Perhaps. (*He moves away.*)

SOPHIE. Marguerite! (*She and MARGUERITE fly into each other's arms.*)

MARGUERITE. Sophie . . . you're back! Are you well, are you recovered? (*She pulls SOPHIE aside, concerned.*)

SOPHIE. Yes, yes . . .

MARGUERITE. (*Looks into her face*) No. You've been ill.

SOPHIE. She left an arm inside me. It festered. It's all right. I've stopped bleeding.

MARGUERITE. You'll need some money. Here — (*She gives SOPHIE her purse*) — no, take it — you'd do the same for me —

SOPHIE. I doubt that.

MARGUERITE. (*Her back to ARMAND, softly*) The man over there, do you know him?

SOPHIE. (*Looks past MARGUERITE*) Yes. (*Sotto voce*) Don't open the door.

ARMAND. Mamselle . . . (*MARGUERITE turns*) . . . your flowers . . .

MARGUERITE. Yes?

ARMAND. (*Gazing at her face*) They're beautiful.

MARGUERITE. Thank you. Camellias.

PRUDENCE. Marguerite always wears them. My dear, may I present Armand Duval?

ARMAND. (*Bows*) Why camellias?

MARGUERITE. Why not?

ARMAND. They have no scent.

MARGUERITE. Ah, but you see, I'm an optimist. (*Gently, as he blocks her path.*) Please don't do that.

ARMAND. I must. When can I see you?

MARGUERITE. (*Smiles*) Please . . .

ARMAND. What do you want? Just tell me what you want.

MARGUERITE. (*Amused*) From you? Nothing. (*She attempts to pass, he prevents it.*)

ARMAND. What's the matter, don't you like me? Tell me what you want.

MARGUERITE. (*To PRUDENCE.*) Such impatience. (*She touches his cheek with a gloved hand, speaks gently.*) Like a child. (*She goes.*)

ARMAND.   No,   wait . . . (*To   PRUDENCE*) . . . you, get her back for me!

PRUDENCE. She won't come.

ARMAND. Why not?

PRUDENCE. For one thing, I think she likes you.

ARMAND. How do you mean?

PRUDENCE. Armand, don't be obtuse. A woman in her position can't afford to like a man. (*ARMAND goes. PRUDENCE looks after him.*) I shall begin to suspect that young man of a romantic disposition.

SOPHIE. Armand Duval? Never!

CLEMENCE. Prudence, supper!

PRUDENCE. Another time, my dears! (*She exits on the arm of DE SANCERRE.*)

(*SOPHIE and CLEMENCE promenade, then swoop down on the Old Duke. CLEMENCE takes the prize and SOPHIE pauses, smoking a cheroot, before leaving alone.*)

SCENE THREE

MARGUERITE's salon. We hear screams, then JAN-

INE, MARGUERITE's maid, runs on pursued by MARGUERITE.

JANINE. I never touched them!

MARGUERITE. Then why were they under your bed?

JANINE. It wasn't me, it wasn't me — leave me alone, Marie!

MARGUERITE. Nothing but trouble from the day you —

JANINE. It's not fair! I was the one found Senor da Costa . . . if it was up to me he'd still be —

MARGUERITE. Well it ain't, so shut your mouth —

JANINE. My nose is all swelled up —

MARGUERITE. The only trouble with your nose is the great, big, gaping hole underneath — come on, where's the rest?

JANINE. Ow! — what?

MARGUERITE. The moonstone collar and the pearls — if you've sold them (*She grabs JANINE by the hair and they grapple, MARGUERITE seeking her jewels. PRUDENCE and PIERRE, MARGUERITE's servant, run in.*)

PRUDENCE. (*Genially*) That's enough — that's enough! (*She separates them with her parasol.*) Pierre! (*PIERRE puts down a pile of hatboxes and hauls the women apart.*)

MARGUERITE. Robbing me from cellar to attic — and you! (*She cracks PIERRE across the face for good luck. To JANINE*) You're going home to your pig-faced mother!

JANINE. (*Throws the stuff on the ground*) Go on, take them! I hope you choke on them!

MARGUERITE. Hang on, where do you think you're going?

JANINE. I'm not staying where I'm not appreciated.

(*To PRUDENCE*) Who was it found Senor da Costa —
Me! (*She goes.*)

MARGUERITE. (*Mutters*) I'll bang her head through
the door . . .

PRUDENCE. They're all the same.

MARGUERITE. . . . well, I've never known a laundress yet that wasn't light-fingered.

PRUDENCE. (*Sotto voce*) You should know dear.
(*Aloud.*) She's right about da Costa, though. (*Marguerite
pulls a face.*) My dear, the uglier the better — they pay
up!

MARGUERITE. I hate her.

PRUDENCE. Yes, well that's because she's a little turd.
But a good maid.

MARGUERITE. Biggest scroungers in the village. I only
took her to show off —

PRUDENCE. Playing the lady? Well, why not? With
those bones there isn't a door you couldn't kick open. I
always had too much flesh. Flesh will take you so far, but
after that it's bones . . . ohh! (*She swoops on a brooch
on the floor*) . . . This is nice!

MARGUERITE. (*Trying on a bonnet, does not turn her
head*) Have it.

PRUDENCE. Really? But they're rubies! . . . (*Puts
them promptly in her bag*) we-ell . . . oh, now that is
enchanting!

MARGUERITE. It doesn't make my face look pale?
(*Displaying the bonnet.*)

PRUDENCE. All the better, class!

MARGUERITE. (*Laughs*) So long as you don't want
ready money —

PRUDENCE. You girls! — never mind, my dear, I'll put
it on your account —

SOPHIE. (*Enters*) What's she up to, getting you in deep again?

PRUDENCE. (*As MARGUERITE laces SOPHIE's stays*) I'm the best friend Marguerite's ever had —

SOPHIE. A leech, you mean —

MARGUERITE. Sssh — (*As SOPHIE crosses, plonks the bonnet on her head.*)

PRUDENCE. Take it off, it makes your face look crooked! (*But SOPHIE has gone.*) You want to watch that girl.

MARGUERITE. Why?

PRUDENCE. For one thing, she coughs.

MARGUERITE. It's nothing serious, cigars that's all.

PRUDENCE. (*As PIERRE enters quickly*) What is it, what do you want?

PIERRE. (*Insolent*) Nothing. (*To MARGUERITE*) The woodman's downstairs, and the upholsterer —

(*MARGUERITE rises with a sigh, finds and gives him money.*)

PIERRE. (*Stands immovable*) There's last month's, and the month's before that —

MARGUERITE. You rogue, I gave you — (*Groans, gives him more money.*)

JEAN-PAUL. (*Runs on fast*) Tan' Marie . . . Tan' Marie! (*He leaps into her arms.*)

MARGUERITE. Jean-Paul! (*She swings him round in ecstasy.*)

MARGUERITE. Yvette! I wasn't expecting you — everything all right?

YVETTE. (*Stolidly*) Yes, thank you, Miss. (*She bobs.*)

MARGUERITE. Your family, your mother?

YVETTE. Yes thank you, Miss. (*Bobs. MARGUER-ITE nods, waits, the boy in her arms, for the girl's unhurried country style. YVETTE smiles. And then remembers the purpose of her visit.*)

YVETTE. Oh — boots. (*She points to JEAN-PAUL's feet.*)

MARGUERITE. (*Puzzled*) Boots. Oh! Oh, you mean he's growing! — oh, you're growing! (*Fetches money, adding more as an afterthought.*) You will put it somewhere safe? (*Yvette nods and bobs.*) Now, my lad, what are we going to get for you? I know — cake!

JEAN-PAUL. Yes please!

YVETTE. Oh good. You said please.

MARGUERITE. Pierre, fetch up some milk and the chocolate cream cake —

PIERRE. You mean the one for tonight? (*She nods.*) No sir, cook'll knife me.

MARGUERITE. (*Giving him a cigar*) Oh go on, Pierre, go on! (*He goes, grinning.*)

PRUDENCE. Don't give him good cigars — you spoil them!

MARGUERITE. (*To YVETTE*) He's well?

YVETTE. Oh yes, been climbing trees, haven't you?

JEAN-PAUL. I saw a squirrel!

MARGUERITE. Oh? Then see what I've got for you! (*It is a carousel. She and the boy sit on the floor watching the carousel turn, like two children. She watches the boy's shining face.*)

JEAN-PAUL. (*Absorbed*) Will it go backwards?

MARGUERITE. (*Absorbed likewise*) No, you'll break it. (*He suddenly leans back, shouts with laughter.*)

JEAN-PAUL. Thank you, Tan' Marie!

YVETTE. That's it.

MARGUERITE. (*Gazing at him hungrily*) Still my little man, are you?

JEAN-PAUL. (*Gravely*) I'm your man. (*He leans forward, hugs her fervently.*)

PIERRE. (*Runs on*) It's the Duke!

MARGUERITE. Where?

PIERRE. On the stairs!

MARGUERITE. Oh, God in heaven . . . (*She hugs JEAN-PAUL, makes a dash, returns to kiss him again, then flies out*) . . . Prudence!

PRUDENCE. Quick, down to the kitchen, little man . . . no, not that way, this way . . . Yvette . . .

YVETTE. What? (*Blundering this way and that.*)

PRUDENCE. Here, quick . . . (*She loads YVETTE with hatboxes*) . . . go on, shoo . . . (*YVETTE runs off.*) Oh, Monsieur le Duc!

DUKE. M' lead horse went lame, so I walked!

PRUDENCE. Bravo, Duke, bravo!

PIERRE. Glass of madeira, your Grace?

DUKE. Why not, why not, why not?

PRUDENCE. (*Sotto voce to PIERRE, who is sneaking a swig behind THE DUKE's back*) You dare!

DUKE. Ah, Janine! (*JANINE swoops on in full regalia.*) And how is our Janine the morning . . . sweet little thing!

PRUDENCE. (*Flat*) Oh adorable.

(*A loud knock. PRUDENCE gestures to PIERRE who hurries to the door.*)

JANINE. (*Covering by arranging cushions behind THE DUKE*) Wicked Pierre, not making you comfortable —

PRUDENCE. (*Advancing with the decanter*) These early

evening visits, so much more satisfying—(*Hisses to PIERRE, who hovers*)—what is it?

PIERRE. The upholsterer. Three hundred francs or the sofa goes. (*PRUDENCE gestures to JANINE to see to it, JANINE flies to the door to soft talk the upholsterer.*)

PRUDENCE. Glorious weather, Duke!

DUKE. Is it, by God?

PRUDENCE. Allow me—(*She makes to refill his glass.*)

DUKE. Steady on, gal, steady on. We don't want to be hors de combat! Eh? What? (*As PIERRE looms.*)

PIERRE. (*Hisses*) Three hundred francs!

(*PRUDENCE flies to the door. The three of them hold it as MARGUERITE enters in a teagown. She saunters over to the DUKE, smiling. He casually hands her a roll of notes. She gives money to JANINE, who pockets a note, gives the rest to PIERRE, who pays the upholsterer and pockets the rest. Behind the DUKE's back MARGUERITE pays PRUDENCE. PIERRE and JANINE leave.*)

MARGUERITE. Mon cher . . . no don't get up . . . (*As the DUKE rises, his eyes following JANINE*) . . . sit—that's an order.

DUKE. Yours to command. (*To PRUDENCE.*) She's so strict with me. I walked!

MARGUERITE. Did you? Then you must be rewarded.

DUKE. Ooh, good, good, good . . . !

MARGUERITE. However, if you haven't been behaving yourself I shall find out . . . let me just say goodbye to Prudence—

DUKE. Ah, Prudence—settling up, eh? Business as usual? D'you still have your little black book?

PRUDENCE. Plus ca change, Duke, plus ca change . . . (*Sotto voce*) . . . the old fool. (*To MARGUERITE*) Shall I say yes to Armand?

MARGUERITE. Armand?

PRUDENCE. Duval. You said he might call.

MARGUERITE. No I didn't. (*THE DUKE hems, she turns.*) Sit! (*THE DUKE sits obediently.*) Oh very well, bring him with the others, damn you. (*PRUDENCE turns to. MARGUERITE suddenly grabs her arm, whispers*) Promise me something. He won't be a nuisance?

PRUDENCE. My dear, you'll manage . . . (*Aloud*) au 'voir, Monsieur le Duc, au 'voir . . .

DUKE. (*Waving her off*) Au 'voir, au 'voir, au 'voir . . .

MARGUERITE. (*Turns to THE DUKE*) Now. Mon cher Hercule. What are we going to do with you, hmmmh?

DUKE. Something special?

MARGUERITE. Something special? Oh, only if you're good.

DUKE. But I am, I am!

MARGUERITE. Are you? No . . . I don't think so. I think you're telling me a lie. And you know what happens to little boys who tell lies, don't you?

DUKE. I am a good boy . . .

MARGUERITE. No . . .

DUKE. (*A sad wail*) I am a good boy . . . I am a good boy . . . (*He takes her hands, smothers them in kisses as she gazes down on his grey head.*) Oh my Camille . . . my lovely Camille . . .

(*He looks up at her, gazing at her face. Gently she helps him to his feet and then leads him slowly from the room.*)

SCENE FOUR

*Later. PIERRE and JANINE come and go, preparing
the room with flowers and trays of drink and glasses.
JANINE pauses to survey the room, bends to rear-
range the flowers PIERRE has set down. He looms
behind her in the low light.)*

PIERRE. Fancy a duck's wing in the kitchen?

JANINE. (*Scornfully*) Hah, if I couldn't do better than
that! — (*But she giggles as he stalks her around the chaise
lounge. He makes a dive up her skirt, she shrieks and
marches off, patting her hair. PIERRE, honour satisfied,
goes, smoothing his hair. A pause, then MARGUERITE
enters. She strolls around the room, inspecting the ar-
rangements, touching pieces of furniture, caressing them
with pleasure, taking her time.)*

MARGUERITE.   My   things . . . my   lovely
things . . . (*She takes another turn and then lies back
on the sofa for a rare moment of privacy and solitude.*)
(*Startled*) I'm happy. (*Puzzled*) Why am I happy?

(*DE SANCERRE, in the shadows, draws on his cigar.*)

MARGUERITE. (*As he approaches and stands behind
her silently*) I'm expecting guests. (*He stands, immovable. She rises, speaks very softly.*) You bastard. (*He
follows her off. Light change.*)

(*PIERRE enters with candelabra. JANINE enters and
hangs about, 'tidying'. PIERRE gestures her off, but
she holds her ground. He grimaces sardonically and
goes. A pause, and then DE SANCERRE enters,
tying his stock.)*

JANINE. (*Soft*) Let me do it, sir. (*She glides forward and, on tiptoe, ties his stock. He nods an abrupt thanks.*) Not at all, Monsieur, anything you wish, Monsieur.

(*DE SANCERRE looks down at her, takes her face in his hand, inspecting it coldly.*)

DE SANCERRE. Bones of a pigeon.

JANINE. Oh yes. I'd crack, ever so easily . . . Monsieur. (*She waits in his path, looking up at him with cool expectancy.*)

DE SANCERRE. You want to be careful.

JANINE. Oh, I'm ever so careful, Monsieur de Sancerre. (*He glares at her dangerously but gives her a note and goes. She exits to bedroom.*)

MARGUERITE. (*As she does so*) Janine!

JANINE. (*Offstage*) I didn't know he was here, how was I supposed to know he was here, I didn't know —

MARGUERITE. (*Offstage*) You devil, how much did he give you, I swear I'll murder you —

(*JANINE runs on with an armful of crumpled sheets.*)

JANINE. How was I supposed to know? (*She crosses and exits. Slight pause. The young COUNT DRUFTHEIM enters, with an enormous bunch of flowers and a package. JANINE returns with fresh sheets and stops short.*) Oh . . . Count . . . what a surprise! (*Flat*) Mamselle will be so pleased.

COUNT. (*Peering over the flowers*) You think so? That is good.

JANINE. Take a seat. Glass of wine? Cognac? (*He shakes his head twice.*) How are you?

COUNT. I am well. Apart, of course, from my heels.

JANINE. What? Oh, yes. I expect they'll get better soon. Did you try the hog's lard?

COUNT. (*Brief*) Yah.

JANINE. Ah . . . you're in for a lovely evening.

COUNT. Oh?

JANINE. Mam'selle's friends are coming to supper.

COUNT. (*Blanching*) Oh, but I thought . . . you said —

JANINE. Never mind. Perhaps they won't stay long. Tell you what, I'll get rid of them for you. (*She stands over him. Taking the point he takes out his purse and gives her a coin.*) Well, I'll try. The trouble is, they'll all be giving me something to let the party run on. If you see what I mean.

COUNT. (*Gives her more and more coins*) This is enough?

JANINE. Oh, aren't you nice! I'm always telling Mam'selle what a sensitive man you are, Monsieur le Comte.

COUNT. Yah, that is true.

JANINE. I know, I just said so. (*Hiatus.*) Oh . . . ah — the weather . . .

COUNT. (*His face beams, all shyness leaves him*) Ah, the weather! This morning was cold, one, maybe two degrees of frost, this is not unusual for the time of year but damaging with these plants which are begun their grow. I am thinking to wear Ulster for the possibility of rain because when I am looking outside window . . . hoop! (*Making JANINE, whose mind has wandered, jump.*) Black cloud! But when I have eaten my good breakfast and performed my exercising, hullo . . . black cloud is no more, but maybe later, so must I wear my good Swedish jacket for sure and — ow! (*As JANINE, bored beyond endurance, clouts him.*)

JANINE. Oh! No, it's all right, I thought I saw a spider in your ear, oh, it's only a bit of fluff . . . ooh! (*She runs round the back of him quickly as MARGUERITE enters, sees THE COUNT, tries to withdraw but is too late. She comes forward with a smile.*)

MARGUERITE. Dear Canute . . . (*JANINE gestures innocently.*)

COUNT. Good evening . . . ah . . . ah . . . ah . . . m . . . m . . . (*he stops, gestures helplessly.*)

MARGUERITE. (*Kindly*) Oh . . . still afflicted? (*The COUNT nods miserably, thrusts the bunch of flowers at her.*)

MARGUERITE. Oh, how lovely—for me? (*Quietly.*) Oh. Chrysanthemums. (*They fall from her hands.*)

COUNT. They are not fresh? But I was assured—

JANINE. (*Picking them up*) They're funeral flowers. For your grave.

COUNT. This is true? In Sweden not so.

JANINE. Well it is here. (*She sweeps them up and goes.*)

COUNT. Forgive me, please. (*He proffers his box.*)

MARGUERITE. It's nothing. (*She opens the box.*) Oh. What beautiful shoes.

COUNT. They are fitting? Please to try.

MARGUERITE. Oh, I'm sure they will.

COUNT. Please to try. (*With an effort.*) My dear.

MARGUERITE. There, that wasn't so difficult, was it? (*He kneels, puts a shoe on her foot reverently. In the second shoe is a diamond necklace.*) Canute? Canute! Oh! They're lovely! (*Jumps up.*) They're like raindrops! Like tears.

COUNT. (*Doing up the necklace*) Yes, as in Sweden when is melting the snow—

MARGUERITE. Yes . . .

COUNT. —first come little drops, plink, plink,

so . . . (*The piano plinks*) . . . yah! and then plink, plink, plink . . . and quickly now . . . plink, plink, plink, plink . . . and running now, plinkety plonk, plinkety plonk . . . (*The piano drowns him*) . . . yah, that is so . . . exactly this! (*He hops into a dance, grasping MARGUERITE firmly. They circle as PRUDENCE and CLEMENCE enter, CLEMENCE with bonbons. The dance ends, THE COUNT out of face.*)

MARGUERITE. The Count was showing me an old Swedish dance — Pierre, a glass of wine for Madame Prudence — (*To PRUDENCE*) — I'll persuade him to teach you.

PRUDENCE. Let him try I'll box his ears. Dear Count, how lovely to see you again — so soon.

MARGUERITE. Clemence . . . you haven't met Count Druftheim, from Sweden. Ma'moiselle Clemence d'Avignon — from Boulogne.

CLEMENCE. What's it called, your dance?

COUNT. It is called — the Hopping Dance. (*He hops, she hops, and she shrieks happily as they dance, ending in a heap on the floor.*)

CLEMENCE. (*Getting up*) I enjoyed that!

COUNT. Yah! Again! (*The piano starts again.*)

PRUDENCE. (*Shrieks*) Enough, enough! (*The piano stops. To MARGUERITE*) My dear, you look enchanting. Duval couldn't keep his eyes off you last night.

MARGUERITE. He wasn't very civil. I hope he means to be more amiable this evening.

CLEMENCE. Armand? He's joining us?

PRUDENCE. If he can tear himself from the tables. At the moment he's enjoying the greatest pleasure in the world, he's winning.

CLEMENCE. (*Arch*) And what's the second greatest pleasure in the world, Count?

COUNT. (*Baffled, after a pause*) Losing? (*She hits him with her fan.*)

CLEMENCE. Come and see the conservatory. The palms are Enormous! (*They move away together. SOPHIE enters, she and MARGUERITE embrace, sit together on the sofa. Light change.*)

MARGUERITE. (*Dreamily*) Well?

SOPHIE. It seems that if you buy the horses you must take the carriage.

MARGUERITE. I must?

PRUDENCE. (*Apart, her feet up*) Sell it.

MARGUERITE. Ye-es. But whenever I sell I lose money. Why is that?

SOPHIE. It's because you're a fool.

MARGUERITE. (*Laughs*) I am?

SOPHIE. My dear, it isn't appreciated, it's despised.

MARGUERITE. (*Puzzled*) What?

SOPHIE. Generosity. (*MARGUERITE rises abruptly and moves apart.*)

MARGUERITE. (*Low with depression*) I'm sorry to hear you say that.

SOPHIE. You should kick me out for a start.

PRUDENCE. (*Lazily*) Amen to that. (*But MARGUERITE, behind SOPHIE, sees something.*)

MARGUERITE. (*Looking at SOPHIE's neck*) Sophie?

SOPHIE. It's nothing. He tried to strangle me. (*Rearranges her scarf.*)

PRUDENCE. She'll end up in the river.

CLEMENCE. Not bored, Count, only with all your travelling you're bound to be debonair.

COUNT. Oh yah.

CLEMENCE. It must be nice coming from a long, thin country like Sweden. Cold though.

COUNT. Oh yah. For example now in Sweden we are

still in the muff and the gaiter, and many degrees of frost.
Also fug.

CLEMENCE. Fug?

PRUDENCE. Marguerite, for God's sake play
something —

CLEMENCE. No! Seven — seven castles?

COUNT. Oh yah —

CLEMENCE. Big ones?

COUNT. Yah, my favourite is Druftenen. Here is the
bestest of all my collections —

CLEMENCE. Collections? Of jewels?

COUNT. No, no, harness of horse and many wheels
and implements of farm, and carriage, and pieces of
makings —

(*MARGUERITE moves to the piano and sings.*)

MARGUERITE.
Should I care more
For my chateau
On the Rhone,

Is the tenderness of stone,
To be preferred,
To the ice
Of your desire —
(*ARMAND enters quietly. She sees him and breaks off.*)
Monsieur Duval? (*She extends her hand.*)

ARMAND. Good evening, Mam'selle Gautier.

MARGUERITE. (*Sings*)
The Major's on the doorstep,
The Colonel's on the stair,
The Brigadier's in the chamber,
His corsets in the air . . .

MARGUERITE.
But here's the cavalry captain,
A galloping at full stride,
With a bump de bump de bump de bump,
To take me for a ride.
(*The others join in.*)
OTHERS.
With a bump de bump de bump de bump,
To take me for a ride.
MARGUERITE.
The Admiral's in the arbour,
The lieutenant's in the hall,
And two or three more outside the door,
And one perched on the wall . . .
But here's the cavalry captain,
A galloping at full stride,
With a bump de bump de bump de bump,
To take me for a ride!
OTHERS.
With a bump de bump de bump de bump,
To take me for a ride!
(*THE COUNT rises and claps fervently, his applause dying before ARMAND's cold stare.*)
PRUDENCE. Hungry, Count?
COUNT. Yah, most hungry.
CLEMENCE. Come on, then. (*Takes his arm.*) What's your favourite, mine's game pie, well, I like everything! There's nothing I don't like!

(*MARGUERITE has a coughing fit by the piano. THE COUNT turns.*)

COUNT. Marguerite is ill?
PRUDENCE. Heavens no, strong as a race horse! (*She

and SOPHIE follow CLEMENCE and THE COUNT.)

MARGUERITE. Monsieur Duval? (*She gestures, to take his arm. But she is taken with another coughing fit. He fetches a glass of water.*) I must have swallowed a feather. (*Hands back the glass.*) Thank you.

ARMAND. Why do you sing that song?

MARGUERITE. You prefer something more sentimental? You surprise me, Monsieur Duval.

ARMAND. Why, have you been studying me?

MARGUERITE. Oh, no more than the door handle.

ARMAND. It doesn't suit you.

MARGUERITE. What would you require me to sing? Something more—elevated? (*Gently.*) Don't delude yourself, Monsieur—(*But the cough overtakes her. AR-MAND gives her his handkerchief. She recovers.*)

ARMAND. Shall I send them away?

MARGUERITE. Of course not! (*She crosses, peruses herself in the glass.*) Heavens, how pale I look!

ARMAND. May I stay?

MARGUERITE. (*Murmurs*) It's impossible.

ARMAND. Why not?

MARGUERITE. Surely I'm not obliged to give you reasons.

ARMAND. Don't you like me?

MARGUERITE. No.

ARMAND. I think you do.

(*And he sits, putting his legs up comfortably, while she stands.*)

ARMAND. What's the matter?

MARGUERITE. (*Surveys him, turns away*) You lack grace, Monsieur.

ARMAND. (*Coarse*) Allow me to put myself in your hands.

MARGUERITE. Why do you seek to be less than you are?

ARMAND. (*Surprised*) You think I should aspire?

MARGUERITE. Who knows, it might be more interesting. Don't tell me you require virtue.

ARMAND. That would be provincial, would it not?

ARMAND. (*Coarse*) Are you going to name your terms, and allow me to fill them?

MARGUERITE. (*Smiles*) What I should require from you is not, I think, yours to bestow.

ARMAND. And what is that?

MARGUERITE. Respect. (*He pulls a face.*) I mean, towards yourself.

ARMAND. Myself?

MARGUERITE. And a little honour.

ARMAND. (*Very cold*) Are you seeking to question my honour?

MARGUERITE. Oh I daresay you keep faith with those of your own sort. I speak of another kind of honour.

ARMAND. And what kind is that?

MARGUERITE. Between a man and a woman.

ARMAND. Ah! You want gallantry?

MARGUERITE. Mere mutual courtesy. (*He grimaces.*) You find that bizarre?

ARMAND. I don't know what you mean.

MARGUERITE. (*Genially*) No. Because you have a black heart. You're a monster.

ARMAND. (*As she moves to go*) Permit me to prove that I'm not.

MARGUERITE. Then begin by allowing me to pass. Which you are preventing. (*He bows, offers his arm.*) Thank you, Monsieur Armand. Why are you smiling? (*For the first time, we see him smile.*)

ARMAND. You called me Armand. (*They walk off. The women run back at once, laughing, followed by THE COUNT, his eyes bandaged. CLEMENCE allows him to catch her.*)

(*Light change. The women lie about. PIERRE enters with an opium pipe. MARGUERITE rises and dances dreamily. She is joined by SOPHIE and they dance in bal musette style, hands on each other's hips. CLEMENCE joins them and the three women drift backwards and forwards, and then separate. The music changes. ARMAND takes MARGUERITE in his arms and they waltz slowly.*)

MARGUERITE. Why?

ARMAND. Because I must.

MARGUERITE. Is it so important?

ARMAND. Yes.

MARGUERITE. (*Soft*) Oh well. If it's so important.

ARMAND. Not if it isn't to you.

MARGUERITE. To me? You *are* sentimental! Such games come expensive in this house.

ARMAND. I don't want to play games. (*The music stops. MARGUERITE steps back.*)

MARGUERITE. Monsieur Armand, what do you want from me?

ARMAND. I want the truth.

MARGUERITE. The truth? Oh I don't think you can afford that.

ARMAND. Nonetheless, it's what I want.

MARGUERITE. Please go away. The Count is waiting, go away with him, please. (*ARMAND shakes his head.*) You see? You are a monster.

ARMAND. If I am, you make me so.

PRUDENCE. Armand, are you coming?

MARGUERITE. Please go away. (*He shakes his head. Pause.*)

MARGUERITE. (*Gently*) Very well. One night, if you insist. (*With a little smile.*) Then you can say that you know Marguerite Gautier, and that she is a disappointment.

ARMAND. Why should I say that?

MARGUERITE. (*Reasonably*) I don't mind what you say as long as you go.

ARMAND. Very well.

MARGUERITE. I have your word?

ARMAND. I promise to do whatever you want. (*She touches his cheek gently, goes.*)

PRUDENCE. Armand?

ARMAND. No. I'm staying. (*He goes. PRUDENCE approaches SOPHIE who turns away and exits. THE COUNT and CLEMENCE kiss gently, and go. PRUDENCE goes.*)

SCENE FIVE

MARGUERITE's bedroom. The room dominated by a most beautiful giltwood bed, carved with flowers, swans and cherubs. Many pillows, edged with heavy lace, and lace on the sheets. A pale blue silk bedcover with padded self embroidery, white camellias and

*white silk tasselling. ARMAND and MARGUER-
ITE are in bed, in low light. ARMAND gasps.
MARGUERITE groans softly.*

ARMAND. (*Softly*) What is it?

MARGUERITE. Nothing . . . nothing. (*She laughs
very softly, lifting her white arms so that they catch the
light. They murmur together. Then silence. Lights to
black.*)

SCENE SIX

The bedroom. ARMAND and MARGUERITE.

MARGUERITE. How many times have you lost your
heart?

ARMAND. None. Until now.

MARGUERITE. Liar. (*Studies his face.*) You must have
been in love. Tell me.

ARMAND. (*Sits up, puts an arm about her*) It's true. I
did love someone once.

MARGUERITE. Who . . . who?

ARMAND. My father's riding master.

MARGUERITE. I'm jealous! Was he handsome?

ARMAND. Not in the least. He was short,
bandy . . . and cursed like the very devil.

MARGUERITE. But you loved him?

ARMAND. Yes.

MARGUERITE. And there's been no-one else? (*He
shakes his head.*) I see. So that's why you're so unhappy.

ARMAND. (*Surprised*) I'm not unhappy.

MARGUERITE. My dear, you're full of grief.

(*She strokes his hair. He turns, gazes at her face, then leaves the bed and prowls round the room, touching her belongings.*)

ARMAND. I love it here. Everything in this room. I love everything you see, everything you touch. I love the glass because it sees your face — I love these — (*He picks up a silver topped bottle.*)

MARGUERITE. Look at the crests, the initials. All different. Remember that when you start to feel sentimental. (*He leaps on the bed, stands over her.*)

ARMAND. Why did you let me stay?

MARGUERITE. Because you were a nuisance.

ARMAND. You could have had me thrown out.

MARGUERITE. Yes.

(*He embraces her passionately. Light change. ARMAND is lying on his stomach in the half light. She caresses his back.*)

MARGUERITE. (*Murmurs*) How well your mother made you . . .

ARMAND. I doubt if she was paying attention at the time.

MARGUERITE. I love your wrists . . . (*Kissing his wrists*) . . . I love your arms . . . (*She kisses his arms*) . . . and oh, I love your back! (*She cuddles against his back, then begins to touch it gently. She explores the nape of his neck, kisses it gently.*) Why is it so moving . . . the nape of a man's neck?

ARMAND. I don't know, I can't see it.

MARGUERITE. (*Laughs, kisses the nape of his neck*) Perhaps it's because you carry all your troubles here . . . and here . . . and here . . . (*Kissing his shoulders.*)

ARMAND. What troubles? (*Kisses her.*) I have no troubles.

MARGUERITE. No troubles?

ARMAND. (*Kisses her*) None at all. (*Light change.*)

ARMAND. (*In the dark*) No . . . now, do it now — no, not like that . . . (*She pulls away from him, he grabs her fiercely.*)

MARGUERITE. What is it, what's the matter with you . . . no . . . Armand, no! (*They fight in the dark.*) What is it?

ARMAND. Nothing . . . it's nothing . . .

MARGUERITE. Tell me!

ARMAND. It's nothing, I've said it's nothing . . . don't let go of me . . . you let me go!

MARGUERITE. You were dreaming . . . a bad dream, you were dreaming . . .

ARMAND. No, no dream . . . I've told you, don't let go of me!

(*She gasps, almost crying out as he grasps her fiercely. Light change. Daylight. ARMAND and MARGUERITE in each others arms.*)

ARMAND. (*Murmurs, after a pause*) Are you hungry?

MARGUERITE. No.

ARMAND. Not even for a necklace in a pair of shoes?

MARGUERITE. Who told you that!

ARMAND. If you wear his diamonds I'll kill you.

MARGUERITE. (*A finger to his lips*) Ssh! I've given them to the Sisters of Mercy.

ARMAND. And the sapphires, and the pearls, and the opals —

MARGUERITE. Despite the unarguable sanctity of my appearance I am not, alas, yet a saint . . . someone has been putting drops in your eyes.

ARMAND.   (*Kisses   her*)   And   for   your mouth . . . (*Kisses her*) . . . this . . . (*kisses her*) . . . all I ask . . . a few simple words in return . . .

MARGUERITE. What do you want me to say?

ARMAND. Marguerite adores Armand. Now. And forever.

MARGUERITE. Would you believe me?

ARMAND. Yes.

MARGUERITE. You'd be a fool.

ARMAND. Say it. (*She whispers in his ear.*) Out loud. Say what you feel.

MARGUERITE. Armand . . . does not displease Marguerite. (*And they leap into each other's arms.*)

(*Light change. MARGUERITE and ARMAND in bed. She turns away. He pulls her towards him. She looks up at him levelly.*)

MARGUERITE. Very well. If you must. (*Slight pause.*) My mother was a laundress, on a big estate. My father died when I was nine. I have four younger brothers. (*Slight pause.*) And I have a son.

ARMAND. (*Slight pause*) You have a child?

MARGUERITE. Yes.

ARMAND. Where is he?

MARGUERITE. With a farmer's wife.

ARMAND. Is that why you, how you came to . . . to be . . . do you live this life because you like it, is that why you —? (*She laughs at him.*) Tell me! I want to know!

(*She leaps from the bed and begins to prowl.*)

MARGUERITE. You want to know. What do you know! I know the way you live, I used to clean the grates with my mother, five o'clock in the morning on tiptoe while you all slept — I saw them, the rugs, the pictures . . . hothouse fruit, warm baths and nine course dinners all a hundred metres from where we lived on potatoes and slept the seven of us together in a coach house loft.

ARMAND. Are you accusing me?

MARGUERITE. No. (*Pause.*) When I was thirteen I became a housemaid. I slept in an attic — my own bed, you can't believe the bliss! After two years Monsieur le Marquis took me into his bed . . . it was his habit with the younger maids. A year later I had our son. (*She plays with the lace on the bed cover. Then she speaks with detached objectivity.*) You have no idea what difference a child makes. Your life is quite changed forever. You're . . . connected. With someone who is, and isn't you. Your own flesh. I love my brothers of course, but, you grow up . . . you go away, you're on your own. Until, if you're a woman, you have a child. Then you are never lonely, you're never alone again . . . whether you wish it or not, whether you see the child or not. It's there. Part of you. Of your body.

ARMAND. Do you —

MARGUERITE. No, I hardly ever see him. He doesn't know I'm his mother. (*Then, as ARMAND starts to speak*) I was dismissed, of course. I went to my mother's sister, where I was not welcome, and sat by the river wondering what to do. The most sensible thing seemed to be to drown myself. (*Pause.*) And then, one morning when I was getting dressed, my cousin came into my room. And started to shake. I didn't have the strength to push him away. Afterwards, he put his fingers to his lips, and gave me a gold coin.

And there it was.

I knew.

All of a sudden. How to do it. How to go through the magic door. How to be warm, how to be comfortable . . . eat fine food, wear fine clothes, read fine books. I had a key, a golden key. (*Laughs.*) After all, what had I got to lose? Innocence? That had gone before I was five. Look at me. I was a pretty child — do you know what that means — it means that when your father's best friend sits you on his lap he puts his thumb in you. Who can you tell, who would believe it? (*She pauses, dreamy.*)

One of the gardeners was kind to us. He asked my mother to send me round for vegetables. It was Sunday, the church bells were ringing, he was in one of the hothouses, pruning the peaches. He said I looked flushed — I was hot, I'd been running. And then he said "Come over here" and sat down on some sacks. So I sat down. And he said "Well, my little maid, are you ready for me yet?" You should have seen the mess. I put up a terrible fight, I had the whole tree down on him, but he took me anyway. He made me get a bucket of water after — to clean up the blood in case the dogs came sniffing.

ARMAND. I'm surprised you don't hate us.

MARGUERITE.. Hate . . . love — (*She shrugs*) anyway, I had a child to support.

(*He shakes her gently to make her continue.*)

MARGUERITE. I took a chance. I went back to the estate — I knew the family were in Paris . . . I let myself in — and I helped myself. I filled a trunk, I took from that profusion what wasn't wanted, needed or regarded. I equipped myself. Then I called up the butler and said that Monsieur le Baron had been kind enough to make provision for me and gave him the name of an hotel I'd found on the morning room table. I fetched my son, took him where I knew he'd be well cared for . . . and I came to Paris! And sat for five days crying for my baby and waiting for the police to arrive. I laid it all out, the dresses, the wraps, the garnets, the turquoises that had never been worn. I sat with my tortoiseshell brushes, my ribbons, the box with the violets from Parma on the lid — oh, you have no idea of the magic of Things when you've never had any!

ARMAND. Well?

MARGUERITE. Nothing happened! Nobody came! So, on a Sunday, with the bells ringing, I put on Milady's yellow dress — and I went out, into the Park!

ARMAND. And?

MARGUERITE. And he was there! Riding! Monsieur le Marquis!

ARMAND. Did he see you?

MARGUERITE. Oh yes.

ARMAND. What did he do?

MARGUERITE. He got down from his horse, and he hit me, in the face. (*Lifting her hair to show him.*) I still have the scar from his ring. (*Slight pause.*) So now you know.

ARMAND. You're a tigress . . . a lion . . . (*But then he looks away.*)

MARGUERITE. 'Nonetheless' . . .

ARMAND. Nonetheless?

MARGUERITE. There is always a nonetheless. Nonetheless, how can I bear it? It's what you all want to know. (*Smiles.*) I bear it very well. Oh at first you shut your eyes, dream of the handsome valet, but then, if you're successful, who has time to think? And who is to say what goes on in our heads?

ARMAND. What do you think of when we make love?

MARGUERITE. Of you.

ARMAND. How can I be sure?

MARGUERITE. You can't.

ARMAND. What is it between us? From the moment I saw you. You accept my ugliness—

MARGUERITE. (*Surprised*) But you're not ugly!

ARMAND. Oh I am. Believe me, I am. (*He studies her face.*) You don't condemn, you don't judge, and yet with you there is . . . what is it? A chance for something other—possibility. (*Looks at her accusingly.*) I'm happy!

MARGUERITE. (*Laughs at his discomfiture*) Is that so alarming?

ARMAND. Unnerving! I'm at home with you. I've never had a home before.

MARGUERITE. You? No home? (*Laughs.*)

ARMAND. I was sent away to school at seven.

MARGUERITE. How could your mother bear it?

ARMAND. I slept in a fourposter large enough for a platoon. She never once came to kiss me goodnight. And only once did she ever touch me. I had forgotten to bow to her as I went to my seat in church.

MARGUERITE. Didn't she love you?

ARMAND. The question never arose.

MARGUERITE. And your father? (*Unobserved, she looks at him with an odd intensity.*)

ARMAND. Like me. A cold devil. What's the matter? You're crying! Don't cry, there's no reason to cry. I've always been perfectly well provided for . . . I am extremely privileged.

MARGUERITE. Oh my dear—(*She strokes his cheek.*)

ARMAND. Don't cry. I don't deserve it.

MARGUERITE. Why not?

ARMAND. I'm worthless.

MARGUERITE. (*Breaks down and sobs*) Don't! Never let me hear you say that! (*She holds him tightly.*) Oh my love . . . it's not right, it wasn't fair—I felt my mother's feet on mine every night of my childhood . . . if I woke she was there, I know her every sigh, her smell, her every murmur . . . you shall never, never, never sleep alone in a dark, empty bed again, I won't have it—oh my love . . . now I know you . . . now I know . . . damn them—damn them all! Armand. I love you.

ARMAND. Ahhh! (*He lets out a great sigh. And another. She strokes the hair from his face, bending over him.*) I never saw the purpose of love before. I never understood its meaning, the purpose of being alive. What possible reason could there be, for any of it? Now . . . now I'm in love with everything . . . with the earth . . . oceans . . . trees . . . even people. Everyone bearable, everything tolerable, because of you. (*She bends and kisses him.*) When you kiss me I come to life.

MARGUERITE. Wake up, Armand. (*She kisses him again. They embrace.*)

(*Crossfade. MARGUERITE sits on the side of the bed putting on her stockings. She coughs a little, sips from a glass of water. ARMAND, aroused by her cough, murmurs.*)

ARMAND. (*Sleepy*) Where are you going?

MARGUERITE. I'm not, but you must.

ARMAND. Why?

MARGUERITE. Because I ask you.

ARMAND. No-one is to touch you.

MARGUERITE. (*Low*) Armand, please. My dear, how can I afford you if—

ARMAND. I can afford you!

MARGUERITE. No. (*He slaps her across the face.*)

ARMAND. I shall give orders that no-one is to enter.

MARGUERITE. Armand, how can you be jealous? You know me for what I am—you know, you knew that about me! Take what you can, what there is.

ARMAND. (*Shakes his head*) That's over, for both of us.

MARGUERITE. For how long? A month, three, six? You think I'd lend you my heart for an instant, I'd be a fool! Don't you know what I'm risking as it is? I'm losing friends, connections . . . I don't know what to do. (*She begins to sniff in real anxiety.*)

ARMAND. (*He can't bear to see her cry, speaks irritably*) Oh stop that.

MARGUERITE. . . . the bank never leaves me alone, there are creditors at the door—

ARMAND. How much do they want, I'll pay—

MARGUERITE. No! The day you pay for me, I'm a dead woman. I can afford you, for a little while at least.

ARMAND. (*Gentle*) Have I not made myself clear? I mean to stay forever.

MARGUERITE. Forever? Oh my dear, however short my life, it will last longer than your love.

ARMAND. You have my word!

MARGUERITE. And what guarantee? Your heart? Can I burn that to keep out the cold? Armand . . . !

. . . this is a house of business! It runs on credit! And let me tell you, when the news that I'm no longer seeing de Sancerre is known —

ARMAND. (*Puzzled*) But you can't bear him.

MARGUERITE. His mother was a Rothschild. I can bear him very well.

ARMAND. I don't believe you. Come away with me, live with me. We have each other, what more do we need?

MARGUERITE. (*Kisses him gently, then shakes her head*) You'd leave me.

ARMAND. What makes you so sure?

MARGUERITE. It's in your interest. As it is in mine to guard my freedom.

ARMAND. Please —

MARGUERITE. No. Don't ask me to be poor again.

ARMAND. (*Slight pause*) Marguerite. I am prepared to change my life for you.

MARGUERITE. And what of my life?

ARMAND. (*Stands formally*) I am asking you to marry me. To be my wife. (*Silence.*)

MARGUERITE. (*Shocked*) You're mad. You don't know what you're talking about.

(*She suddenly finds the whole thing excruciatingly funny, starts to giggle, and then laughs and is unable to stop.*)

ARMAND. (*Rallies*) Very well. Since you find the idea ludicrous, we won't marry! It's all the same to me. Don't you understand . . . don't you understand — we're free! To do as we please! (*He embraces her.*) Too much love, that's what it is, too much love . . . (*He kisses her.*) What can I do for you . . . what can I give you?

MARGUERITE. Nothing, nothing.

ARMAND. Nothing?

MARGUERITE. (*Laughs*) To hear myself say so! I can't believe it. What do we need, you and I? (*As he bends to kiss her a thought strikes him.*) What is it?

ARMAND. How unbearable, to be any other man on earth.

MARGUERITE. (*Touches his face*) Or any woman.

ARMAND. I'll arrange everything. (*She shakes her head.*) Why not?

MARGUERITE. My dear, they won't let us.

ARMAND. They can't prevent us!

MARGUERITE. Oh . . . if I could. If everything were different . . . no. There is no world, no way that you and I can connect except in the moment. Please . . . (*Sadly*) . . . no, don't touch me. There's nothing for us. I could look over the wall at you all my life and never get to touch your coat-tails. Don't be a fool, Armand. Only a fool believes a lie. (*She turns away, and tries to stifle a spasm. But begins to cough.*)

ARMAND. Stop it. Stop it! (*She gasps at his harshness.*) Breathe! Breathe, damn you — you can if you choose! (*She tries. They breathe together. But then she turns a blanched face to him with a faint smile, gestures helplessly . . . and haemorrhages. He leaps for a napkin, she grasps it urgently. And hands it back. It is red. Silence but for her breath.*)

MARGUERITE. (*Whispers, as he makes to kiss the napkin*) No! . . .

ARMAND. (*Snarls*) Now will you listen to me?

MARGUERITE. (*Whispers*) It's from the throat. The doctor assures me . . . it's not the relentless form of the disease.

ARMAND. There's been blood before? (*She nods. They*

cling together. A pause.) We'll go away, to the country. We find a house, and walk and sit in the sun — think of it, buttercups in the meadows, the woods full of bluebells — find a coat, come away this minute —

MARGUERITE. Oh if it were possible . . .

ARMAND. Marguerite, who decides, if not us —

MARGUERITE. A house with a barn, and poplar trees . . .

ARMAND. What do we own, if not our lives? What else are we responsible for?

MARGUERITE. And we would eat stewed rabbit, and eggs, and cherries, and all the things they eat in the country —

ARMAND. I mean it! Live, Marguerite — Live! You can . . . if you choose!

MARGUERITE. (*Tired*) Choose? . . .

ARMAND. Yes. Choose. (*Gently*) Demand it. Please! Come away with me now, I know the very spot, it's high, with wide open fields and oh, the air — you'll breathe!

MARGUERITE. Can you promise?

ARMAND. Yes!

MARGUERITE. Perhaps for a month, six weeks —

ARMAND. No, not like that! Can't you see, YOU must decide! For yourself! Make the choice!

MARGUERITE. (*Exhausted*) Very well, if it's what you want . . . no, I understand. I . . . choose. (*He buries his face in her shoulder in triumph. Above his head she smiles sadly, unconvinced.*)

ARMAND. You see? Was it so difficult? So simple. (*He lifts her gently onto the bed.*) All you had to do was — (*But he suddenly springs back away from her, his face terrified.*)

MARGUERITE. What is it?

ARMAND. (*Staring at her, his face shocked*) Your eyes!

MARGUERITE. What's the matter?

ARMAND. I can't see your eyes!

MARGUERITE. Ssssh . . . (*She opens her arms to him.*) . . . oh my dear—it's nothing . . . a trick of the light, that's all . . . (*He comes into her arms and she holds him, consoling him. They embrace.*) Ohh . . . could it be possible? A life together?

ARMAND. (*Murmurs*) Why not?

MARGUERITE. A dream . . . (*She strokes his head.*)

ARMAND. No . . . real . . . (*They embrace, clinging together.*)

MARGUERITE. Oh my love . . .

ARMAND. What else is it all for?

MARGUERITE. My love . . .

ARMAND. What else?

Camille

ACT TWO

SCENE ONE

A graveyard at night. ARMAND and GASTON enter.

ARMAND. What time is it?

GASTON. (*Consults his watch*) Nearly two. They will be here in a moment.

ARMAND. You must be tired.

GASTON. No. I am wide awake.

ARMAND. Nonetheless, I have exploited your good will.

GASTON. My dear sir, I am a lonely man. If it has been of the least assistance for you to tell me your story, why then I am more than delighted to miss a few nights sleep. My only wish is that you would abandon tonight's endeavour.

ARMAND. Where is the grave?

GASTON. Here. She must have been well loved.

ARMAND. What?

GASTON. So many flowers. My dear Armand, I beg you, come away. What object now . . . what point?

ARMAND. Why was this done?

GASTON. It appears that the obsequies were arranged by friends . . . women friends of the deceased.

ARMAND. So they put her here.

GASTON. My dear Duval, what difference where she lies? There's a fine plane tree — the view is good —

ARMAND. It's unacceptable.

GASTON. Is it not more appropriate that she lies here, in this simple spot? You've told me of her life, will she not be happier . . . more comfortable . . . with those of her own kind . . . ordinary people, people she knew and understood and had affection for? You think she would prefer a grand vault, all on her own . . . alone? Is that what you truly believe? (*Voices, off.*) They're coming. (*An inspector arrives with the gravedigger and a workman.*)

INSPECTOR. (*To GASTON*) Monsieur Duval?

ARMAND. I am Armand Duval.

INSPECTOR. Good evening, sir. Fine night. (*He clears his throat.*) You have the written permission? (*ARMAND gives him a paper. He scrutinizes it by the lantern.*) And the certificate? (*He reads this too, hands it back.*) This you retain. The other we keep. Very well. Open the grave.

(*The diggers remove the flowers and the planks.*)

GASTON. (*Draws ARMAND aside*) It's still not too late. Tell them to stop, I beg of you. At least come away!

ARMAND. No.

(*The men bring up the coffin.*)

INSPECTOR. (*To ARMAND*) You understand, sir, that it is my duty to have the coffin opened in case of request for removal of remains. The law demands that we identify the corpse. (*ARMAND nods. The gravediggers open the coffin. They step back, put handkerchieves to their faces. ARMAND groans.*) Get on with it, man!

(*The workman unloops the shroud, revealing the body.*

ARMAND cries out. GASTON holds him but he breaks away.)

ARMAND. No, no, no, no, no! (*He backs away, pushing his scarf into his mouth. He staggers. GASTON supports him. Whispers*) Her eyes . . . where are her eyes?

INSPECTOR. Sir? You identify the remains?

ARMAND. (*Breaks away from GASTON*) No! No, no, no!

No! (*He leaps, to grasp the body. They push him away. He goes, followed swiftly by GASTON.*) No . . . no . . . no . . . (*Lights to black.*)

SCENE TWO

ARMAND's rooms. A large open trunk. PIERRE enters with clothing for packing.

ARMAND. (*Offstage*) Pierre . . . Pierre? (*Enters, throws a pair of boots to PIERRE. As he goes*) Shirts?

PIERRE. Already in the trunk. (*He exits separately. Pause. ARMAND's father enters. He moves about, inspecting. PIERRE enters, jumps.*) Monsieur?

FATHER. Is my son here?

PIERRE. Monsieur le Marquis?

FATHER. You know who I am?

PIERRE. (*Takes his hat and gloves*) Yes Monsieur, indeed, Monsieur.

FATHER. Tell him I'm here.

PIERRE. At once, Monsieur. What will you take, Monsieur?

FATHER. Coffee and brandy. (*Pierre goes. He exam-*

ines the trunk. ARMAND enters.) Ah, there you are. Good morning to you.

ARMAND. An early call.

FATHER. Late more like from the looks of you. Fine morning. I've been trying a new horse — a black rig, I believe I shan't take him. (*ARMAND gets dressed.*) I hear you distinguished yourself again at the tables last night. (*ARMAND bows ironically.*) A few more such triumphs you'll be the first bankrupt of the season.

ARMAND. I fancy Lady Luck is about to smile on me.

FATHER. You can't seriously mean that you're gambling to win?

ARMAND. Somewhat lacking in style I agree.

FATHER. And the swiftest course to ruin. Thank you. (*To PIERRE. He drinks.*) Ah — good sort of cup of coffee.

ARMAND. What do you want? (*He takes papers, reads them briefly.*) You find these unclear?

FATHER. My dear Armand, if you wish to realise capital —

ARMAND. The money is mine, to dispose of as I wish —

FATHER. Your   mother's   will   was   perhaps ill-advised —

ARMAND. I am in need of funds.

FATHER. (*Nods to PIERRE to go*) So we are led to believe. What are you doing out there in your love nest — burning it to keep warm?

ARMAND. Marguerite has debts.

FATHER. The best kept woman in Paris?

ARMAND. Be careful.

FATHER. The money's running out like the Rhine. (*ARMAND packs, without answering. His FATHER watches.*) I realise we've never been close —

ARMAND. An understatement.

FATHER. Nonetheless —

ARMAND. What was it you used to call us, my brother and me? Ah yes. "This is the heir . . . and this is the spare."

FATHER. A joke! (*Slight pause.*) Nonetheless . . . we are alike, you and I. On the surface, nothing given away . . . underneath, boiling rage. You see — I know! (*As ARMAND, despite himself, looks up, grimacing.*) I do understand. Placed as we are . . . no-one to believe, no-one to trust . . . take your pick between the craven and the crafty — yet one must have warmth. To buy affection . . . to pay . . . the cleanest bargain, the most honourable transaction. Everything clear and understood and in its place — I absolutely concur. The right woman — a beauty of course, intelligent, sympathetic, discreet . . . a woman of wit and style . . . and to find one with generosity of spirit . . . if you'll allow me, may I say I admire your taste —

ARMAND. Have you finished?

FATHER. You know I'd care for you to hear me out. There is no objection to your taking a permanent mistress. On the contrary. However — in our position one must beware the wire, eh . . . the low branch. Can't afford to take a fall. Responsibilities.

ARMAND. Any responsibilities I care to assume will be of my own choosing.

FATHER. Ah, the Bohemian life — well, why not, for a while. Time enough for the halter.

ARMAND. What do you want?

FATHER. To arrange your affairs for you. I have come to settle your debts — and to offer you a draft for twenty thousand francs.

ARMAND. That's remarkably generous.

FATHER. In return we ask only that you maintain the lady discreetly and in a manner which will not embarrass your family.

ARMAND. I see. (*Returns to his packing.*)

FATHER. Surely that's generous?

ARMAND. A fair bargain, you mean?

FATHER. If you wish to put it that way.

ARMAND. (*After a pause*) There is something I think you should know. I intend to marry Marguerite. (*A silence.*)

FATHER. That — as you know — is entirely out of the question.

ARMAND. She says the same. Nonetheless, that is what I intend to do.

FATHER. (*After a pause*) I forbid it.

ARMAND. You can't prevent it.

FATHER. Can't I? (*Pause. He sits, seemingly tired.*) Armand. None of us is here by choice. We are all of us random cards. We play the hand dealt. If I'd had my choice I'd have been a gamekeeper. I should like to have bred animals — however, there it is.

(*ARMAND smiles at him sardonically*).

ARMAND. Forced to submit to privilege! My condolences.

FATHER. My dear boy, you are my heir. Responsible for estates the size of Provence —

ARMAND. The land is not entailed, let my brother have it —

FATHER. Impossible. (*Slight pause.*) Have you no thought at all for your family? (*ARMAND grimaces.*) Do we mean so little to you? Do you want to break your sister's heart — her engagement has just been announced, De Luneville will break it off at once, what's to happen to the poor girl? It's a love match. He's in love with her.

ARMAND. If it's a love match he'll marry her.

FATHER. And destroy himself? You know better than that.

ARMAND. (*Mutters, after a pause*) You don't begin to understand.

FATHER. Understand what?

ARMAND. I have to marry her.

FATHER. Why?!

ARMAND. It's my only chance.

FATHER. Chance?

ARMAND. For life.

FATHER. Life? What sort of life? You intend to create a new universe above the aspirations of the rest of us, is that it? What do you think marriage is . . . some sort of beatified love affair, impervious to the winds that blow? It's a contract! Look around you! You think Society runs on Love?! Talk to me of love in six months when the money's run out.

ARMAND. Once our debts are settled—

FATHER. Once her debts are settled she'll leave you.

ARMAND. (*Slight pause*) Six months ago I should have agreed with everything you say. Now, I'm the most fortunate man in the world because Marguerite Gautier loves me. Because Marguerite Gautier is prepared to spend her life with me. It is not a question of love, though that goes without saying. It is a question of friendship. Of respect.

(*His FATHER turns, in a towering temper.*)

FATHER. Respect? Respect?! For a whore?! You dare to talk of love . . . you dare to speak of friendship—

with a whore? You dare to come to me—talk of marriage? Introduce a harlot into my family? Are you seriously suggesting that you want as your life's companion, before God and the church, as the mother of your children . . . as our heirs . . . a woman who has felt the private parts of every man in Paris? (*He almost stumbles as ARMAND makes to lunge at him, recovers himself.*) Good God, boy, what does it matter, one woman's slot or another?

ARMAND. I warn you. Don't speak of her.

FATHER. (*Pause*) Very well. I shall stop your allowance and disclaim responsibility for your debts. If I post that publicly you may whistle for credit, there won't be a door left open to you. My dear Armand, think it over. (*ARMAND does not reply. His FATHER goes to the door.*) Come and see me tomorrow. I shall be at home at three o'clock.

(*He goes. PIERRE gives him his gloves and hat. There is a hurried conversation, the Marquis gives PIERRE money and goes.*)

ARMAND. Pierre? . . . Pierre! (*As PIERRE arrives quickly.*) What is it?

PIERRE. Nothing, sir, nothing.

ARMAND. Good. Are we ready? (*Eager to go, he helps PIERRE off with the trunk.*)

SCENE THREE

A Garden. MARGUERITE and JEAN-PAUL strolling. He carries a cage with two doves. They lie down to inspect them.

MARGUERITE. Have you chosen their names?

JEAN-PAUL. Oh yes.

MARGUERITE. Well? What are you going to call them?

JEAN-PAUL. The little one's named Snowy, and the big one's named Plump, after Madame Prudence.

MARGUERITE. You rogue! (*She chases him, AR-MAND enters, catches JEAN-PAUL as YVETTE enters with JEAN-PAUL's jacket and a basket.*)

MARGUERITE. (*To JEAN-PAUL*) Now be careful with the eggs.

YVETTE. He's as careful as can be, aren't you — he finds them quicker than me!

MARGUERITE. Wear your jacket.

JEAN-PAUL. No, it's too warm —

ARMAND. Oh, let the boy be, he doesn't need —

MARGUERITE. Just to be sure — (*But ARMAND waves YVETTE off.*)

YVETTE. (*Happily*) Come on! Race you to the barn!

JEAN-PAUL. Yes! (*He races off, followed by YVETTE who screeches happily. A pause.*)

ARMAND. At last. (*She turns to him.*) I have you to myself.

MARGUERITE. You're jealous? Ah, you're jealous! (*He kisses her.*)

ARMAND. Of course. (*Kisses her.*)

MARGUERITE. Don't be jealous.

ARMAND. Not if you ask it.

MARGUERITE. Are you happy? (*He nods.*) Yes? You're sure?

ARMAND. Ye-es.

MARGUERITE. What is it, what's the matter . . . there's something wrong — oh, tell me!

ARMAND. No. It's nothing.

MARGUERITE. (*A wail*) Tell me!

ARMAND. I've been misled.

MARGUERITE. What do you mean? I haven't misled you — oh, I have never sought to mislead —

ARMAND. Not by you. By Love.

MARGUERITE. Love?

ARMAND. I have been entirely misinformed.

MARGUERITE. You are disappointed? Ah . . . you are disappointed.

ARMAND. No, not disappointed.

MARGUERITE. What then?

ARMAND. (*Gazes down at her tenderly*) I had no idea. I had no idea.

MARGUERITE. It's a dream.

ARMAND. (*Shakes his head*) Real! (*Kisses her face.*)

MARGUERITE. Happiness? No . . . too much . . .

ARMAND. I know what you mean. To be the custodian of something so precious . . . what to do . . . how to keep it safe —

MARGUERITE. We can't . . .

ARMAND. We can. We will. (*Takes her hand. They sit.*) Marguerite they cannot hurt us. There is no way they can pull us apart. We're strong, you and I . . . engines of possibility. (*He takes her hand.*) I shall do as we planned — become a printer . . . write, if I've the talent for it, if not, print the works of those who have. It'll be as we've said — we'll work together, side by side — without ambition, except to excel . . . without greed, except to offer the best of ourselves. (*He kisses her fingers.*) Our aim must be to find our true work — to live, to support our children . . . to read, to think . . . and to be as clear as we can. (*They embrace tenderly for a still moment.*) I love it when we're alone. I love it when we're not — I watch your face, your hands, your smile — but when we're alone, you're mine —

PRUDENCE. (*Followed by CLEMENCE and SO-PHIE*) So this is where you're hiding!

MARGUERITE. Prudence! — how lovely! (*She greets them.*) Clemence — oh my word, what pearls, they're as big as pigeons' eggs!

CLEMENCE. I know, they keep you ever so warm!

PRUDENCE. (*Sourly, to MARGUERITE, aside*) Bought by the Count, for you.

CLEMENCE. Yes, we had a laugh about it — you don't mind, do you, Marguerite? There, I knew you wouldn't. I knew we'd still be friends . . . anyway, all the best friends are where you never see each other.

MARGUERITE. (*Embraces SOPHIE*) Sophie . . .

SOPHIE. You're well?

MARGUERITE. As you see, blooming.

SOPHIE. So it suits you, country life?

PRUDENCE. Wait till the winter and the mud.

CLEMENCE. Chilblains —

SOPHIE. Ice on the washing water!

PRUDENCE. They'll be back. (*Laughter.*)

ARMAND. (*To CLEMENCE*) And how is the Count?

CLEMENCE. Wonderful, we've been travelling!

MARGUERITE. Where?

CLEMENCE. Heaven knows, we kept having to be somewhere to get to somewhere else. I think it was the Mediterranean but I was so busy drinking it all in.

PRUDENCE. They were asked to the Royal costume ball — Clemence and the Count!

MARGUERITE. Really!

PRUDENCE. (*Resigned*) She went as a powder puff, he went as a brush. (*The others laugh at her social disappointment.*)

MARGUERITE. But you like him?

CLEMENCE. Oh yes, he's so interesting about his estates and his railroad company and his shipping fleet —

ARMAND. WE have a pond!

CLEMENCE. A pond — ooh, good, can we punt, is there a boat?

ARMAND. Afraid not.

CLEMENCE. Never mind. People in boats are such hooligans. (*She and SOPHIE follow ARMAND off.*)

MARGUERITE. (*After a pause*) How much?

PRUDENCE. Ten thousand.

MARGUERITE. Is that all?

PRUDENCE. Marguerite, selling is not buying.

MARGUERITE. You saw the Duke?

PRUDENCE. Nothing. (*YVETTE enters with a tray of drinks and fruit. PRUDENCE assesses her shrewdly.*)

MARGUERITE. (*Noticing, smiles*) Janine left me. She didn't take to country life again. I told her you might find her something.

PRUDENCE. I already have. (*Slight pause.*) My dear, how long can this go on?

MARGUERITE. For as long as the money lasts.

PRUDENCE. What then? The landlord's repossessed.

MARGUERITE. But there was cash in hand!

PRUDENCE. All gone. I can't get credit in your name any more. Even the little woman you set up in the glove shop gave me her account. There are new stars rising. If you continue this nonsense I shall be forced to abandon you.

MARGUERITE. (*Low*) I thought we were friends.

PRUDENCE. Friendship is based on good sense. You can't expect the rest of us to follow you to ruin. For God's sake, Marguerite, do you want to end up like me, everybody's catspaw? There's nothing so vacated as being a woman of my age. Take my word for it, what you have doesn't last forever.

MARGUERITE. I know. (*Pause.*) He's asked me to marry him.

PRUDENCE. Has he, by God? So that's why his father's back from Biarritz.

MARGUERITE. He's in Paris?

PRUDENCE. Duval didn't tell you? You'd be a Marquise of course but there's no profit in it the way things stand. You'd have to leave France, he'd go into drink — I've seen it all before.

MARGUERITE. I don't think so.

PRUDENCE. (*Looks at her shrewdly, then*) You love him — is that it?

MARGUERITE. Perhaps.

PRUDENCE. Good, then you won't want to ruin his life. He'll be ostracised, cut off from everything he knows. What about your family, your brothers, just lifting their heads above water, thanks to you . . . your mother, she's not getting any younger . . . and then there's the boy, the one who calls you Tan' Marie, you want him schooled, don't you? You're a beauty. Men desire you. You keep us all afloat, servants, seamstresses shoemakers . . . not a bad achievement for a little girl who couldn't write her name. My dear, don't throw it all away. (*Slight pause.*) What are we all to do, how do we survive, without you? (*Slight pause.*) Listen. I've met this charming wine merchant. He saw you at the opera and he's dying to make your acquaintance. Not young, but very soundly based. You could still see Armand — why not? He must learn to share! You'll afford him a lot longer if you give up these foolish notions of love in the attic. My dear, I know these aristocrats. They're cold. Finished off in the cradle.

MARGUERITE. He's changed.

PRUDENCE. I doubt that. I doubt that very much. Come back. I'll hire a new carriage for you with a pair of matched bays . . . once it's known that Marguerite Gautier is back in Paris . . . new address, new wardrobe — my dear, you should see the silks this year, colours like light, you won't be able to resist them! Come back.

MARGUERITE. Prudence . . . I truly appreciate your coming to see me —

PRUDENCE. But you're not coming back?

MARGUERITE. No.

PRUDENCE. We'll give it another month. (*Marguerite shakes her head with a smile.*) Very well. If you change your mind let me know. Au revoir, I don't want to drive in the middle of the day, the horses will get hot. (*She goes. SOPHIE enters.*)

MARGUERITE. (*Over her shoulder*) No, don't call me a fool. (*She looks up.*) How's Paris?

SOPHIE. Amusing. Marguerite! Why ruin yourself?

MARGUERITE. (*Smiling*) Particularly for Armand Duval.

SOPHIE. You really like him. You like Duval.

MARGUERITE. (*Low, aside*) There seems to be some sort of necessity. I am — almost persuaded — some of the time. (*Turns, smiling*) Amazing as that may seem.

SOPHIE. (*Slight pause*) I'm thinking of going away.

MARGUERITE. Oh — where?

SOPHIE. Egypt.

MARGUERITE. Who with?

SOPHIE. (*Shrugs*) A man.

MARGUERITE. Do I know him? (*SOPHIE shakes her head.*) Is it practical?

SOPHIE. If you mean can he afford it — oh yes.

MARGUERITE. Why? (*But SOPHIE does not reply. Low*) Will he treat you well?

SOPHIE. Oh I doubt it. But I daresay I shan't behave either. (*They laugh, and sit together.*)

MARGUERITE. You're looking well.

SOPHIE. Thank you. Are you coughing? (*MARGUERITE shakes her head.*) Good. Then life here suits you?

MARGUERITE. (*Doubtfully*) It seems so. (*They drift off together, arm in arm. Light change. Calls softly*) Jean-Paul . . .

(*The party return, replete with Sunday lunch, and sit in the warm afternoon sun on cushions. A pause. Someone sighs with pleasure.*)

JEAN-PAUL. I know—colours! A!

MARGUERITE. Ohh . . . let me see . . . amber.

JEAN-PAUL. B.

SOPHIE. Blue.

JEAN-PAUL. C. I know, I know, I know! . . .

ARMAND. (*His head heavy with wine*) Hey . . .

JEAN-PAUL. Crimson!

MARGUERITE. Good! (*She pokes ARMAND, but he lies on his back.*)

JEAN-PAUL. D.

CLEMENCE. D . . . D . . . ah—dark blue.

JEAN-PAUL. That's two words!

CLEMENCE. Oh all right, doughnut then!

JEAN-PAUL. Doughnut's not a colour!

CLEMENCE. Yes it is, it's a sort of yellowy, sugary, buttery kind of brown, everybody knows what colour a doughnut is, silly . . . how Old are you?

JEAN-PAUL. (*Crushed*) Seven.

CLEMENCE.. (*Scornful*) Is that all?

SOPHIE. Oh come on, whose turn is it? Jean-Paul — you go —

JEAN-PAUL. But are we having food?

MARGUERITE. We ought to have a policy —

CLEMENCE. Oh, let's not have policies, we don't want policies —

SOPHIE. All right — we accept doughnuts. A,b,c,d,e . . . E . . .

ARMAND. Elephant . . . eggcup —

JEAN-PAUL. (*Furious*) Stop it! (*Bursting into tears*) He's not playing right, he's not playing it right! (*He hits ARMAND with a pillow, MARGUERITE does the same.*)

ARMAND. All right . . . pax . . . all right. (*Whispers to JEAN-PAUL*) Emerald.

JEAN-PAUL. (*Big smile*) Emerald. (*They all clap him. Slight pause.*)

MARGUERITE. Flame.

SOPHIE. (*Slight pause*) Garnet.

CLEMENCE. Garnets come in lots of colours.

ARMAND. Rejected!

SOPHIE. Oh . . . grey — ginger — golden!

JEAN-PAUL. Hurray! (*Slight pause. CLEMENCE sighs.*)

CLEMENCE. H. Oh, I thought of one just now . . . now I've forgotten it.

SOPHIE. Double marks to me if I give you one?

CLEMENCE. (*Daunted*) Oh, we're not having marks, are we?

(*A slight pause.*)

ARMAND. (*Lying on his back, hands behind head,*

speaks quietly) H. House . . . home . . .
happy . . . (*He takes MARGUERITE's hand.*)

(*Light change. JEAN-PAUL moves to stand with
YVETTE for the farewells. CLEMENCE kisses
him. MARGUERITE kisses CLEMENCE goodbye. SOPHIE caresses JEAN-PAUL, MARGUER-
ITE turns to SOPHIE.*)

MARGUERITE. Write to me. (*They embrace fondly.
JEAN-PAUL and YVETTE go inside. SOPHIE goes.
MARGUERITE looks after her then comes forward to
ARMAND, who picks up his gloves, ready to leave.*) Must
you go?

ARMAND. A few matters to settle.

MARGUERITE. But I've spoken to Prudence, we shall
survive!

ARMAND. You may depend on me for that. (*He takes
her in his arms.*)

MARGUERITE. Must you see him?

ARMAND. My father? I said I would.

MARGUERITE. Be careful. Don't let them persuade
you. (*She covers her anxiety in a hug, laughing.*) And if
you dare to go near the tables I shan't speak to you for a
week!

ARMAND. A week! (*Kisses her.*) My solemn word.
Don't wait up for me.

MARGUERITE. You know I shall.

(*They embrace once more and he goes. MARGUERITE
paces, her arms about her, concerned. JEAN-PAUL
runs on, followed by YVETTE.*)

JEAN-PAUL. Tan' Marie, Tan' Marie . . . we're going to catch frogs!

MARGUERITE. (*As he runs past*) *You* didn't finish your lunch!

JEAN-PAUL. (*Calls back*) It was only the cabbage!

YVETTE. It was only the cabbage! (*MARGUERITE smiles, watches them go. ARMAND's FATHER enters behind her.*)

FATHER. There was no-one to announce me so I took the liberty of walking round. (*MARGUERITE turns to face him.*) Good God, if it isn't Marie!

MARGUERITE. (*Bows, cold*) Monsieur le Marquis.

FATHER. Well. (*He laughs.*) Good-day to you. (*MAR-GUERITE moves to the table, rings a small bell. PIERRE appears promptly.*)

PIERRE. Monsieur le Marquis?

FATHER. Fetch me some Armagnac and water, would you?

PIERRE. Yes, M'sieu. At once, M'sieu. (*He goes quickly.*)

FATHER. Pretty spot. (*He advances, gazes at the view.*) Fine view of the river. Damned hot dusty drive, though. (*PIERRE returns. THE MARQUIS mixes his drink to his satisfaction. To MARGUERITE*) Fine old Armagnac, can you afford it?

MARGUERITE. We keep it for creditors.

FATHER. Not a lot left.

MARGUERITE. As you see. (*THE MARQUIS nods to PIERRE, who leaves.*)

FATHER. I hear you're being sold up.

MARGUERITE. And what are you going to do about it?

FATHER. I? Not my affair. If my son chooses to ruin himself that's his concern.

MARGUERITE. But how is he to live?

FATHER. How indeed, since he's cashing up, it seems, on your behalf.

MARGUERITE. I have not asked him to do so. I've tried to prevent it.

FATHER. So much so that he's gone through his mother's inheritance in a month. A pity, since I'm withdrawing financial support . . . including my name to his bills.

MARGUERITE. You can't!

FATHER. The disclaimers are in my pocket.

MARGUERITE. He has as much right to the money as you have. You didn't earn it.

FATHER. Come, losing your temper? Wearing thin already, is it?

MARGUERITE. You'd like to believe so.

FATHER. No pleasure for me watching my heir make a fool of himself before the whole of Paris . . . let alone upsetting his family.

MARGUERITE. So you've come to offer me money.

FATHER. Of course.

MARGUERITE. How much?

FATHER. Fifty thousand.

MARGUERITE. You have a sense of humour.

FATHER. I'll go to seventy-five.

MARGUERITE. You're wasting your time.

FATHER. A hundred then — that's the top.

MARGUERITE. Have you got it with you?

FATHER. Don't play the fool with me girl. There's a closed carriage outside, to take you back to Paris. Come with me now, I'll pay the rest of your debts and set you up again. Come . . . Marie . . . be honest — aren't you bored, after Paris? It won't be so pretty in the winter.

(*Pause.*) Armand will understand — if not now, later. (*Slight pause.*) You cannot stand by and see him ruined if you truly and genuinely love him.

MARGUERITE. (*Low, her head bent*) How could I wish to ruin him?

FATHER. I knew you would see the right of it. We know the rules, you and I. Come, take my arm —

(*He bends, touches her arm. She springs away from him as if burnt.*)

MARGUERITE. No! Don't touch me. Every day, every night I've feared it . . . lying awake, waiting . . . No more of it. That's over for me. You have no authority here.

FATHER. No authority? (*Laughs.*) I could have you arrested within the hour —

MARGUERITE. On what charge?

FATHER. Does it matter? Do you think you matter? You will leave with me now. That is what I wish, and that is what —

MARGUERITE. Go away . . . get away from me —

FATHER. Don't get hysterical —

MARGUERITE. What right have you to come here threatening me under my own roof, do you think I can't take care of myself? You think because I'm a woman you can come here and bully and threaten? You think I'm nothing? A piece of wood to be pulled out of the road? We're free of you and your kind. We don't need you. You poison the air you breathe, the ground you walk on, so take your foul breath and your rotting teeth and your stinking ass out of my house . . . go on . . . get out —Get Out!

FATHER. Have you gone mad?

MARGUERITE. Get out! . . . get out . . . get out! (*She picks up a knife.*)

FATHER. I can have your name placed on the list of undesirables. If I do that —

JEAN-PAUL. (*Running on*) Tan' Marie . . . look! . . . (*He stops at the sight of a stranger. MARGUERITE freezes. She waves YVETTE to take the boy away. But THE MARQUIS approaches.*)

MARGUERITE. Don't touch him!

FATHER. That's a fine frog, my boy. A fine frog like that deserves a louis. (*He takes a coin from his pocket, gives it to the boy.*)

JEAN-PAUL. Thank you, sir — ooh, a gold one! (*He turns in delight to show YVETTE.*)

FATHER. (*To YVETTE*) Boy's a credit to you. (*He offers YVETTE a coin, she takes it with a bob.*)

YVETTE. Ooh, thank you sir, ever so, sir.

MARGUERITE. Take him in, Yvette. (*They go. Silence.*)

FATHER. A fine child. Your son?

MARGUERITE. Leave him out of it.

FATHER. Good looking boy. A little rough in his speech, perhaps, but that's soon mended.

MARGUERITE. He is not your concern.

FATHER. Is he not? He lives with you here? With you and my son? (*She does not reply.*) I see. What plans do you have for him?

MARGUERITE. Our plans are none of your affair.

FATHER. I'm merely thinking of his future. As you well know, a boy needs decent schooling. Which is not cheap.

MARGUERITE. Will you go? (*She is suddenly exhausted.*)

FATHER. No, a fine boy. I'm taken with him. (*Laughs*) He has an air of Armand at the same age — no, I'm taken with him.

MARGUERITE. Go. Just go.

FATHER. You've given no thought to his future? You surprise me . . . no, no, no, of course you have . . . the boy is obviously well cared for. I congratulate you. However, he'll need a patron. I wonder. I might even be prepared to assist . . . in the matter of an education.

MARGUERITE. Thank you, no.

FATHER. Surely the offer is worthy of thought. What is his future to be, hawked about with you and my son, not a sou between you? Two years schooling if he's lucky? Come, my dear, you're a realist, you know how most people live, you must know the worth of such an offer. Do you want the boy ending up a labourer in the fields, with an aging mother to support?

MARGUERITE. I tell you no.

FATHER. I might even be prepared to take him . . . accept him as my natural son . . . after all, in a way it's his birthright. We'll hire a tutor, start him on his declensions.

MARGUERITE. You devil. You're a devil.

FATHER. He'll be reared as a gentleman.

MARGUERITE. (*Low*) You think I want him to be like you?

FATHER. You want him able to read, don't you? Think for himself, carry on a profession? Keep a decent household . . . lead a civilised life? It's in your hands, Marie. It's for you to choose. What shall it be? Will you choose for yourself? Or for the child?

MARGUERITE. No . . . no . . .

FATHER. After all, I am the boy's father.

MARGUERITE. No!

FATHER. I see. You prefer to choose for yourself, put your own selfish wishes before the future of your own child, hardly surprising from a woman of your sort —

MARGUERITE. No, that's not true!

FATHER. No more than to be expected —

MARGUERITE. I can't, I can't give him up! I won't.

FATHER. Very well. In that case I shall be forced to get a magistrate's order stating that you are an unfit mother. I can have that child removed from you before sundown —(*His voice now loud and very frightening*) Good God, woman — what do you think you're playing at? Have you forgotten your Place?!

MARGUERITE. No, don't . . . please don't, no you can't . . . no, please . . . oh, please sir . . . no, please . . . (*She begins to weep and laugh hysterically. JEAN-PAUL runs on followed by YVETTE, MARGUERITE clasps him feverishly.*) No, please . . . oh, please . . . please . . . please . . . (*Holding the child she reaches out to THE MARQUIS.*) No — No! (*As THE MARQUIS takes the boy.*)

FATHER. Take the boy away. (*YVETTE, frightened, obeys him.*)

MARGUERITE. (*Weeping*) No . . . no . . . (*She weeps. THE MARQUIS waits for her to subside. But she doesn't.*)

FATHER. For Heavens sakes, Marie! (*Mutters*) No need to make a fuss. (*She weeps, sobbing now inconsolably.*) Be reasonable! Take what you can get! (*The weeping turns into heavily drawn breaths. MARGUERITE begins to cough.*) You were always a realistic girl. Courageous too, as I remember — I admired your spirit. (*MARGUERITE sniffs. Despite herself, she coughs again.*) Surely you would rather know where the child was placed? . . . it goes without saying I shall keep my word on the matter. Come . . . you're known as a generous woman. (*He fetches her a glass of water. She sips and gasps, getting her breath. And then a long silence.*)

MARGUERITE. (*Speaks at last in a low, thick voice*) I want him educated.

FATHER. As I've said.

MARGUERITE. And you'll adopt him — give him your name? (*THE MARQUIS nods.*) I don't want him left to servants!

FATHER. I am about to marry again. I believe she is fond of children.

MARGUERITE. (*A moan*) Oh please . . .

FATHER. He will be well treated, I assure you.

MARGUERITE. Shall I . . . shall I see him again?

FATHER. Perhaps, when he is a man. Let time create him for us. Then we'll see. A fine child. I congratulate you. (*He offers his arm.*) Come. We'll go into the house and you can write the note.

MARGUERITE. The note?

FATHER. To Armand. Saying that you have returned to Paris. That you are bored with the country, that you prefer your former existence. There must be no confusion, no doubt as to your intentions. I must have your assurance that you will never seek to receive my son again. Do I have that promise? (*She lowers her head.*) Good. After you have written the letter we will drive into Paris together, and then the boy can come home . . . with me. (*He helps her inside, takes hat and cane from PIERRE and goes. Light change. PIERRE enters with a garden lantern. A pause. ARMAND enters.*)

ARMAND. Marguerite . . . Marguerite?

(*PIERRE steps forward with the letter. ARMAND reads it and falls to his knees, muttering feverishly.*)

SCENE FOUR

The foyer of the opera house. CLEMENCE enters, fuming, followed by COUNT DRUFTHEIM.

CLEMENCE. I tell you *I* wouldn't stand for it!

COUNT. My Snowdrop, you are not enjoying the opera?

CLEMENCE. Letting him pester her like that, it really riles me!

COUNT. But my beloved, it is the makings up, not the true . . . and the singing, so full and round —

CLEMENCE. Well it makes me go outraged —

COUNT. Beloved —

CLEMENCE. She should punch him in the head!

COUNT. You have the soft, warm heart!

CLEMENCE. We'll go again tomorrow, see the rest . . .

COUNT. No, we will not. You shall choose.

CLEMENCE. I would have enjoyed it more only one of my stays went and I lost the drift a bit.

COUNT. Ping, ping! (*PRUDENCE enters with JANINE, now dressed to kill.*)

JANINE. But we'll miss the ending!

PRUDENCE. Nonsense, what do you care, anyway I've seen it, she kills herself. What happened? Where did he go?

JANINE. (*Sulky*) He's at the bar.

PRUDENCE. Now why did you allow that, you fool —

Clemence! Count! What a wonderful surprise! Wicked! When did you arrive?

CLEMENCE. Yesterday.

PRUDENCE. And you didn't leave me a note — how well you look — don't they look well, Olympe!

JANINE. Yes, like a couple of Parma hams. What? (*As PRUDENCE slaps her.*)

CLEMENCE. Janine, is it you, you look wonderful! We saw every country in Europe except Japan!

JANINE. (*Making conversation*) Really? Did you see Venice?

CLEMENCE. Oh yes — but it was flooded.

COUNT. Madame Prudence, you are from the opera? So fine, is it not?

JANINE. (*To fill the breach as PRUDENCE pulls a face*) Oh yes. Miserable though.

COUNT. Yah, yah, so depress. First we see the young girl, so happy and innocent. But who is coming here? It is the baritone, what does he —

PRUDENCE. (*Quick*) How was your voyage?

CLEMENCE. Lovely, every minute of it. (*She and THE COUNT smile soppily.*)

PRUDENCE. You enjoyed yourselves then?

COUNT. Yah, yah. (*To PRUDENCE.*) Now the first day was warm, but not so warm that we are without the yackets. Then on the second day is coming little shower . . . (*PRUDENCE gives a little shriek and flees, pursued by THE COUNT*) . . . the third is more rain, but not so —

JANINE. How are you getting on with him?

CLEMENCE. We're like roosting hens, you should see us!

JANINE. I told you, didn't I? Who put you up to it, remember?

CLEMENCE. (*With a triumphant nudge*) I know! (*She gives JANINE one of her bracelets.*) He's ever so clever, Janine.

JANINE. (*Busy with the bracelet*) Well I said so, didn't I?

CLEMENCE. Mind you, he does eat an awful lot. Still, I expect that's to feed his mind.

JANINE. (*Giggles*) Yes, build it up. (*They burst into giggles.*)

CLEMENCE. You'll never guess what he polished off tonight? Half a side of venison! (*She belches, easing her stays.*) I had the other half.

JANINE. (*As COUNT enters*) Count, over here . . . no, it's me, Janine . . . don't you remember? Only I'm called Olympe now. (*Giggles.*) You'll never guess who's paying My bills! (*To THE COUNT.*) How did you find Italy?

CLEMENCE. It took a week or two.

COUNT. Florence is a most beautiful city, with many works of art which of course we have seen all . . . twice.

JANINE. Good! I hear you've been eating well.

COUNT. Oh yes. The food is ripe, but it is not so agreeable to look up and see swimming before you in the river rats . . . also cats . . . sometimes swimming and sometimes dead. (*PRUDENCE enters, wheels, but too late.*) Ah, Madame Prudence! As I was saying . . . ninethly, on the matter of disposals of sewage —

CLEMENCE. Sophie! (*As SOPHIE appears in a striking Arabic dress.*) You're back!

PRUDENCE. My dear! (*Embraces SOPHIE.*) How was Africa?

SOPHIE. The most exciting place in the world — except Paris!

PRUDENCE. Splendid, now the season can begin — my

dears, we must go shopping. Pale is the thing this season, oh yes, pale is the last word!

DUKE. (*Enters*) Pale eh? It will suit La Gautier then! Hahaha!

PRUDENCE. Dear Duke, always the wit . . . tra la la!

SOPHIE. (*Draws PRUDENCE aside*) What is it, is Marguerite ill?

PRUDENCE. Never more sparkling.

SOPHIE. She's ill.

PRUDENCE. I haven't said so. You should see the Russian bear she has in tow.

SOPHIE. How ill?

PRUDENCE. Skin like watered milk.

SOPHIE. What is it — opium . . . the lungs? Tell me! (*ARMAND enters. SOPHIE turns.*) Well. Armand Duval.

ARMAND. (*Bows*) Ah, a blackened face from the past . . .

JANINE. (*Taking his arm*) Armand, we missed you!

SOPHIE. What's this? (*And, as JANINE whispers in ARMAND's ear*) I see.

JANINE. You look surprised.

SOPHIE. Me? Not in the least, I assure you.

JANINE. Do you like my dress?

SOPHIE. You look like a firework.

PRUDENCE. Such a handsome couple. Olympe, so full of life! . . . he adores her!

SOPHIE. (*To ARMAND*) Do you — adore her?

ARMAND. She is disgusting.

PRUDENCE. Armand, stop it.

SOPHIE. What's the matter with him? (*There is a sudden hush. SOPHIE turns. MARGUERITE, wearing a black and gold dress, with a little embroidered veil over her eyes enters, accompanied by a heavily built and or-*

nately dressed Russian. SOPHIE steps forward to see and is shocked by MARGUERITE's appearance.) God in Heaven!

PRUDENCE. Quick, he mustn't see her — (*SOPHIE shrugs, it is too late.*)

ARMAND. (*Bows*) Good evening. Up for a breath of fresh air, Mam'selle Gautier?

MARGUERITE. (*Low*) Monsieur Duval. (*She bows, tries to pass.*)

ARMAND. How are you tonight, Prince — (*As THE PRINCE staggers*) — ah, out of action I see. (*Helps him to a chair.*) I compliment you on your choice of transaction, Mam'selle . . . the elderly, the hors de combat — a convenient clientele —

JANINE. Well if it isn't Marie! Oh, don't you look old! Armand, come and dance . . . I could dance all night, you won't tire *me* out!

ARMAND. (*As he dances, calls to THE PRINCE*) You'll find the lady wanting, Prince . . . failing in contractual commitment —

PRINCE. (*In Russian*) Clear out of it before I kill you . . . (*The company dance. THE PRINCE then rises majestically, sweeps MARGUERITE in his arms, spins with her wildly. They both crash to the floor.*)

ARMAND. (*Clapping*) Throw them some buns! Come on, Mam'selle, let's see the rest of your tricks!

JANINE. Oh, don't waste your time, Armand! (*The music stops and her voice rings out in the silence*) Who wants yesterday's mackerel? (*SOPHIE glides across the room. JANINE screams and tries to evade her. The two girls fight, rolling over and over. Apart, MARGUERITE rises.*)

ARMAND. (*Approaches her at once*) You're leaving us, Mademoiselle Gautier?

MARGUERITE. (*As he blocks her path*) Don't, please . . .

ARMAND. Another assignation, no doubt . . . who is it? Honoré de Sancerre waiting with his whips and his costume trunk? (*He holds her.*)

MARGUERITE. Armand, there's no point. (*Low*) Please let go.

ARMAND. The monster obliges. (*But as he steps back and bows he sways. She steadies him. In each other's arms, they cannot move.*)

MARGUERITE. No Armand . . . please . . . (*She looks up at him. For a second it seems that they will embrace. Then he draws back, and cracks her across the face. The waiters and THE COUNT run to her assistance and pull him away.*)

COUNT. No, sir, no! Please!

PRUDENCE. Armand, for God's sake!

COUNT. Come away, please . . . come away . . . sit . . . here, please . . .

JANINE. (*Bursts into noisy tears*) Armand . . . Armand . . . !

PRUDENCE. (*clouts her*) Shut up, you.

SOPHIE. (*To MARGUERITE*) Are you all right? (*She helps her up.*)

DUKE. (*Advancing*) What's going on here? What's going on? (*SOPHIE helps MARGUERITE past him to the exit. As they pass he shakes his head.*) Too thin . . . too thin!

CLEMENCE. Oh Armand . . . (*Silence.*)

PRUDENCE. That was ill-done.

ARMAND. I beg your pardon. Deepest apologies.

PRUDENCE. She is ill.

ARMAND. So am I. (*He lurches to his feet, to leave. Turns.*) You're killing her.

PRUDENCE. I? (*Turns to the company, laughing.*) He thinks he's a saviour! You think to rescue Marguerite Gautier — oh, that's a well-trodden path, my friend. (*He goes. She calls after him*) Perhaps she prefers her freedom! (*Silence. Laughs*) What a diversion. (*To JANINE*) Come, my dear. I have it — we'll go to the Varietes' — call the carriages! Monsieur le Duc? (*She invites him to take JANINE's arm.*)

DUKE. Anything to oblige, Prudence, anything to oblige . . . (*He grabs JANINE eagerly and they follow PRUDENCE off.*)

PRUDENCE. Let's see what Paris has to offer! (*They go.*)

CLEMENCE. But why did he do that? He shouldn't have done that.

ACT TWO

SCENE FIVE

MARGUERITE's bedroom. MARGUERITE in bed, SOPHIE on her feet.

SOPHIE. I'll kill him. With cyanide.

MARGUERITE. My dear, no you won't.

SOPHIE. He hit you!

MARGUERITE. Yes! (*And her eyes are shining. SOPHIE observes this, advances on her.*)

SOPHIE. Oh don't you dare to tell me you —

MARGUERITE. (*Laughs*) Of course not, it's over — he was drunk. We'll go shopping tomorrow?

SOPHIE. If you wish.

MARGUERITE. I can't seem to do without it these days.

SOPHIE. We could drive out to Malmaison — the air will do you good.

MARGUERITE. I'm perfectly well.

SOPHIE. Are you? (*Slight pause.*) Have you thought of going south?

MARGUERITE. (*Quick*) Oh I couldn't leave Paris!

SOPHIE. Why not? You should think of your health, if not for yourself, for the boy.

MARGUERITE. I . . . I've had him adopted.

SOPHIE. What?!

MARGUERITE. So, as you see, I don't see him any more.

SOPHIE. (*Shocked*) But, why did you do that?

MARGUERITE. At least he'll be educated — it's more than we were.

SOPHIE. Is it? Well I wouldn't have let him go . . . I'd rather he was a pimp than let him go if he was mine!

MARGUERITE. Well he isn't, so there's an end of it.

SOPHIE. (*Wails, childish*) I liked playing with him!

MARGUERITE. (*Low*) Have one of your own then.

SOPHIE. Hardly likely, after all the knitting needles. (*They look at each other with brief grins. A silence.*) Damn you, get over it.

MARGUERITE. (*Low*) Tell me how.

SOPHIE. (*Jumps up*) I knew!

MARGUERITE. Oh, stop scowling like a cross pekinese.

SOPHIE. My dear, forget him, you don't need him, how could you allow yourself — we'll go away. Together. Where is Jean-Paul, I'll fetch him back — for God's sake, there are bruises all over your face! (*Noises off. PRUDENCE enters, pushing past YVETTE.*)

PRUDENCE. I'm not intending to stay, girl, oh what a

fracas . . . the whole of Paris is talking! Are you recovered, you look very pale, pinch her cheeks Yvette!

MARGUERITE. I'm fine. Yvette, a glass of cognac for Madame Prudence.

PRUDENCE. Clemence sends her love, I've left them below, she's a goose, but my dears, more sense than I gave her credit for — she's going off to Sweden as his Countess! I daresay he's been turned down by all the Swedes, well, half a minute and you're gasping but she thinks he's a wit, they're studying wasps now. She's all right? . . . you're all right? — good, because the Prince is on his way up. I told him he was the one who slapped you, it does no harm. He's bringing them with him.

MARGUERITE. (*Alarmed*) Who?

SOPHIE. Who?

PRUDENCE. The emeralds, you fools! Tiara, necklaces, bracelets — the whole parure! I told you it could be done! All I got from the drunken beast was niet, niet, niet so I said they were out of fashion, that you'd never wear them — he's had them all reset — especially for you! (*Laughter off.*) I'd better go before they turn your place upside down — heavens, what a noise they're making . . . I'll be in in the morning to settle up — keep out that brandy bottle, you'll have no trouble . . . (*She goes, blowing a kiss.*)

SOPHIE. (*Slight pause*) How much are they worth?

MARGUERITE. The emeralds? Millions.

SOPHIE. Good. We'll leave in the morning and find a place in the warm where the sun shines every day, why not? We'll have the sun on our backs for the rest of our lives — what's to prevent us? (*Bends to kiss MARGUERITE.*)

MARGUERITE. (*Pulls back*) Better not.

SOPHIE. Tomorrow! (*She goes quickly. MARGUER-*

ITE sinks back, exhausted. YVETTE enters with a covered pot. MARGUERITE spits into it.)

MARGUERITE. Have they all gone?

YVETTE. Yes, Madame. Is there anything I can get you, Madame?

MARGUERITE. Oh yes, a shawl please Yvette — it's so cold!

YVETTE. Cold? But the room's — (*She bites her tongue, gets a shawl, puts it gently about MARGUERITE's shoulders.*)

MARGUERITE. You're so good to me. (*Murmured.*)

YVETTE. Shall I go for the doctor?

MARGUERITE. Why?

YVETTE. There's no need to pay, he'd come for you.

MARGUERITE. But I don't need him . . . I'm well, I'm very well.

YVETTE. Then may I bring supper?

MARGUERITE. Oh — no thank you.

YVETTE. Please, a little soup . . . just a little . . .

MARGUERITE. (*Exhausted*) Well, if you must . . . (*YVETTE runs off, pleased. A slight pause. Then ARMAND enters.*)

ARMAND. What's the matter, she ran down the stairs like a weasel.

MARGUERITE. The silly girl has a soft heart, that's all.

ARMAND. You look pale.

MARGUERITE. It's nothing.

ARMAND. I didn't hurt you. Did I hurt you?

MARGUERITE. No, I'm just cold.

ARMAND. Cold? The room's stifling — (*He puts out a hand, touches her cheek, recoils.*) You're icy!

MARGUERITE. It's nothing. (*She rises, sits at dressing table, away from him. He prowls.*)

ARMAND. The room! It's exactly the same! I thought

everything had been sold?

MARGUERITE. I managed to buy back some of the furniture. The rest I had copied.

ARMAND. Why?

MARGUERITE. I wanted everything to be the same. (*Pause.*)

ARMAND. (*Low*) I should like to burn this room and you with it.

MARGUERITE. (*Slight pause, very low*) Do it, then. (*Pause.*)

ARMAND. All a lie. All those days . . . all those nights . . . coming up for air, not just from love, but from the ecstasy of talk . . . all nothing . . . Do you know what I've been through. I'm a dead man. Look at me. I'm uglier than before. At least before there was no possibility.

MARGUERITE. Forget me—survive, I'm useless to you! If I truly loved you the best thing I ever did was let you go.

ARMAND. Is that it? You thought you'd ruin me?—

MARGUERITE. No. it's as I said in my letter. I was bored, I'd had enough—

ARMAND. I don't believe you. Look at me—look at me! Do you know what it's cost me to come to this house? . . . what am I doing in this room?

MARGUERITE. Don't . . . (*She weeps*) . . . don't . . .

ARMAND. No, don't do that. (*He holds her urgently.*) Oh my love . . . my own love! How could you . . . if you knew! I've been dead . . . everything dry, everything smelling of metal in my head . . . I see, I hear people's voices but I'm cut off—I'm not part of it any more . . . (*He clings desperately, like a child*) . . . please . . . oh, please . . . please, please, please . . .

MARGUERITE. No, you mustn't, no, you don't understand —

ARMAND. Please, please, please let me in — please, oh please . . . (*He looks up at her.*)

MARGUERITE. (*Groans*) Ohh! Oh your dear, beautiful face! Oh I can't! (*And she embraces him.*)

ARMAND. My own love . . . never let me go . . . (*They embrace and kiss feverishly.*)

MARGUERITE. Oh my love, my love . . . (*They kiss.*)

ARMAND. Why, why did you do it . . . why?

MARGUERITE. I did it for Jean-Paul.

ARMAND. Why? Where is he?

MARGUERITE. I've lost him. I had to give him away. And as you see, I have lost you both.

ARMAND. We'll get him back, go away, away from here —

MARGUERITE. My dear, how are we to live?

ARMAND. What does it matter, the rest is unimportant! We'll go away together, the three of us . . . our own life . . .

MARGUERITE. Oh yes! Oh if —

ARMAND. We will — we'll go . . . we'll go to Italy, see the paintings — Michelangelo, Botticelli . . . (*Kissing her hands*) . . . I'll never leave you —

MARGUERITE. No, never —

ARMAND. We'll see the hill towns, Siena . . . Perugia . . . oh — and Venice — we'll see Venice — my love, you're so cold!

MARGUERITE. No, I'm warm —

ARMAND. Together there is nothing we may not achieve —

MARGUERITE. Oh my love . . . (*YVETTE enters, coughs discreetly.*) What is it?

YVETTE. (*Softly*) It's the Prince, Madame.

ARMAND. Send him away.

MARGUERITE. Yes, send him away! No . . . wait . . . (*She turns to ARMAND*) together? Do you mean it?

ARMAND. We must leave . . . now!

MARGUERITE. There IS a way . . . (*She walks apart, turns, her eyes shining.*) Oh my love . . . emeralds! Rivers and rivers of emeralds . . .

ARMAND. (*To YVETTE, apart*) Tell him to go.

MARGUERITE. Why not? A chance . . . a possibility! Allow ME to find a way for us — oh I will, I can, I must!

ARMAND. No.

MARGUERITE. But don't you see? It's not important! — he'll fall asleep on the carpet — (*She crosses, brushes her hair swiftly*) — oh my love, I bring you a dowry — *I* shall provide for us . . . why not? We'll travel — we'll see Italy! . . . feel the sun on our backs for the rest of our lives! . . . oh, I feel so well! We Shall have our lives! Trust me . . . will you trust me? (*ARMAND looks up at her, face blank with shock. He shakes his head slowly.*) Not for one night?

ARMAND. (*Murderous*) Be careful . . . oh, be careful . . .

MARGUERITE. (*Slight pause*) But I am. I was. I have been — so careful. I guarded our love like a fragile flame. And I was right, for that is what it is. (*She slides down to the floor by the bed. He rises.*) No! Don't go. (*But he turns away, picks up his coat and approaches her as she kneels on the floor.*) It's for your sake! (*He reaches into the pocket of his coat.*) No, Armand, no . . . (*She clings to his legs*) . . . please . . . please, you can't go — not now . . . no . . . no . . . (*But he pulls a handful of notes from his pocket and showers her with money. And turns and walks out.*)

(*MARGUERITE, shocked, remains on the floor for a prolonged moment. She seems to be hardly conscious. Then, at last, instinctively, she begins to scrabble for the money, clutching it to her. She rises, and lurches towards her dressing table. And has a massive hemorrhage.*
YVETTE rushes in to assist her. She helps MARGUERITE out of the room.)

SCENE SIX

The chaise lounge, dressed in white. MARGUERITE enters alone, drifting like a ghost. She pauses by the chaise longue, and then lies down.
YVETTE enters, and sits by MARGUERITE. The bailiff comes to the door and YVETTE rises quietly, crosses to him and shakes her head. There is a whispered altercation, but the bailiff brushes past YVETTE, who goes, and begins to price the furniture. He reaches the bed.

BAILIFF. Mam'selle? With your permission?

MARGUERITE. (*In a cracked voice, whispers*) How much for me?

BAILIFF. Beg pardon?

MARGUERITE. (*Sighs*) Not a lot. (*The BAILIFF moves away. He continues to price the furniture quietly. SOPHIE enters, with the priest and YVETTE. She and YVETTE stand by as the priest performs the ritual. MARGUERITE at first seems unconscious, but the touch of the priest's fingers on her brow arouses her. She flinches, becomes aware of his presence and makes small noises, trying to push his hands away. SOPHIE and YVETTE placate her.)*

MARGUERITE. (*To SOPHIE*) I'm not dying, am I?

SOPHIE. Of course not. (*The priest finishes the ritual and steps back into the shadows. SOPHIE and YVETTE move into the background and the rest of the company appear severally. Only MARGUERITE'S breathing is heard. Suddenly it falters. She half rises and calls, in a maternal, warning tone*)

MARGUERITE. (*Her voice cracked*) Jean-Paul? (*She sinks back, exhausted. Only her breathing is heard, becoming more broken and urgent. MARGUERITE dies.*)

SCENE SEVEN

The Tuileries Gardens. Very early on a beautiful spring morning. ARMAND and GASTON appear. ARMAND looks about him.

ARMAND. It's daylight.

GASTON. Yes. A beautiful morning.

(*PRUDENCE appears with CLEMENCE, THE COUNT and JANINE.*)

PRUDENCE. Is it —? Armand, what a surprise, I didn't recognise you! We were all certain that you were abroad —Clemence, Count, over here! (*She looks at GASTON with interest, nods.*) Monsieur?

GASTON. (*Bows*) Gaston de Maurieux.

PRUDENCE. What weather! (*Offering her hand to be kissed.*)

COUNT. Ah, the weather —

JANINE. Yes, makes you glad to be alive . . . what? (*As CLEMENCE pushes her, jerking her head towards ARMAND.*) Oh. (*She and CLEMENCE and THE COUNT eat sweets throughout.*)

PRUDENCE. Mon cher Armand, where have you been hiding? We've been making our plans, for the summer —

JANINE. We're off to Sweden!

PRUDENCE. We're all going north, for the nuptials.

CLEMENCE. Join us!

COUNT. (*Slight bow*) We are delighted. (*ARMAND does not reply.*)

GASTON. I believe that Monsieur Duval wishes to remain in Paris.

CLEMENCE. Through the summer?

JANINE. He'll die of the heat!

PRUDENCE. Why not come north — new scenery, new faces —

GASTON. Your friends are right. Go to Sweden . . . I believe it's a fairy tale in summer —

COUNT. Most beautiful, I assure you.

ARMAND. Thank you, no.

GASTON. Then where you will. I should be delighted to accompany you if you'd care to — Spain . . . Switzerland for the mountains — I have it, Italy! We'll go to Italy, see the hill towns . . . Siena . . . Perugia . . . Venice, we'll go to Venice — Venice, my dear fellow —

(*ARMAND breaks down and weeps. The others are shocked into silence. CLEMENCE moves towards ARMAND, but PRUDENCE puts out a hand.*)

PRUDENCE. No. Leave him to me. (*She stands apart*

from ARMAND, and lets him cry for several beats.) Ah, my friend . . . no more rapture? Well . . . can it last? At least you had it, for a while. What more do you want? What more is there?

ARMAND. (*Looks up*) You. You did it. You finished us. It wasn't the thing, was it? Were we so threatening? One man? One woman? No. It wasn't convenient. The wrong transaction.

PRUDENCE. What are you—

ARMAND. No profit in it. Nothing to be sold— nothing to trade—so we must be done out of it. (*He rises.*) There was a chance, for something real . . . something honest, ordinary—there for the taking like an apple on a tree . . . but you don't want that, do you?

PRUDENCE. What's the matter with him?

ARMAND. So tell me, what do you want? What is it that you want from us?

PRUDENCE. Is he drunk?

ARMAND. After all . . . we're your creatures. You make us. So tell me, what do you want from us? Tell me!!

PRUDENCE. (*Evades him, then turns, light*) Very well, you wicked boy. Armand—(*She hooks an arm through JANINE's, draws her forward.*) Be nice to Janine—Olympe.

(*Silence.*)

ARMAND. (*Quietly*) You make us ugly.

PRUDENCE. I? (*She laughs.*) I make you ugly?

ARMAND. A monster. (*And his look stops her in her tracks. Quietly.*) Very well. (*He looks round at the others.*) If that is what you want. (*He goes. Silence. THE COUNT and CLEMENCE stop eating.*)

PRUDENCE. Eh bien, mes braves . . . a little beauty

sleep! Monsieur Gaston, my card. Call on me — no, I insist! I am at home every afternoon at five. You need enjoyment — you see? I can tell. Trust Prudence. Canute? Olympe? The Countess — where's the Countess?

(She descends on CLEMENCE and THE COUNT and
shepherds them away with a last, charming wave to
GASTON.
JANINE lingers, under her parasol, then smiles at GAS-
TON, and goes.
GASTON watches them go. He looks at the card, and
slips it into his waistcoat pocket. He looks up at the
new day, and goes slowly. Lights to black.)

O.S.L.

1. 2 Crumpled Sheets — Janine Iiii
Ashtray — DeSancerre's exit Iiii
SM.RND.TABLE: Iii-Iiii
    Tray w/ Madeira decanter (full) — top off
    2 wine glasses
    Silver tea set on bottom shelf.
Tray — Pierre IIi
    Coffee pot (½ full) — top off
    Brandy decanter (½ full) — top off
    Demi-tasse cup
Tray — Pierre IIii
    Armagnac decanter (small amount) — top off
    Water Pitcher (½ full)
    1 glass
2 Anisette glasses (½ full) — Clem/Soph IIii
Frog jar w/ frog — Yvette IIii
Bowl soup/spoon — Yvette IIv
2. 4 Hat boxes (2 practical) — Pierre Iii
Towel — Pierre Iii
Pink BonBon box w/ bonbons — Clemence Iiii
Wrapped Crysanthemums — Druftheim Iiii
Shoe box (cream shoes — diamond necklace in left shoe)
    — Druftheim Iiii
Maroon bonbon box — Clemence IIii
Ledger/pencil — Appraiser IIv

D.L.VOM

Tray — 3 glasses champagne (½ full) — Nick Ii
Tray — Janine Iiii
    Wine decanter (full)
    Water pitcher (not practical)

1 water glass (½ full)
2 wine glasses
OVAL TABLE: Iii-Iiii
   Objet d'Art on top
   Humidor w/ 3 cigars on top
   Wrapped Carousel on bottom shelf — Iii
DRESSING TABLE: Iiv-Iv
   Vanity things glued down.
   Hand mirror on right
   Hanky on right
   Brush on left
   Tortoise barette on left
   Perfume bottle on left
Lacy Peignoir — Marguerite Iv
Cotton Peignoir — Marguerite IIiv
Black Shawl — Marguerite IIiv
Pair boots/tan socks (to be pre-set) — IIi
Pair boots (to be packed) — Armand IIi
GARDEN TABLE — IIii
2 GARDEN STOOLS — IIii
Tray — Yvette IIii
   Fruit (oranges, grapes)
   2 lemonade drinks (½ full)
   1 glass water (½ full) — Marg.
   1 packet medecine (powd. milk)
   1 spoon   1 bell
   1 KNIFE
Riding crop — Pierre IIii
Egg basket — Yvette IIii

O.S.R.

Tray — 3 champagne glasses (½ full) — Dave Ii
Champagne Bottle (¼ full) — Armand Ii
Candelabra/matches — Pierre Iiii

2 Cigars/matches — DeSancerre — Iiii
Ashtray
SM.RND.TABLE: Iii-Iv
   Clock/ashtray/gold box on top
   Horse on bottom shelf
   8 franc notes in drawer — Marg. Iii
BED: Iiv-Iv
   white fitted sheet
   white flat sheet
   4 pillows w/ white cases
   fancy bedcover
Letter — Pierre IIii
2 glasses champagne (½ full) — Dave IIiii

D.R.VOM

Hookah — Pierre Iiii
Tobacco/matches (for hookah)
Black Lace Scarf — Druftheim Iiii
Black Scarf — Sophie Iiii
2 Folded Sheets — Janine Iv
Tray — Janine Iv
   Bottle Champagne (¼ full)
   2 champagne glasses (¼ full)
   bowl of grapes
Tray — Janine Iv
   Coffee cup (¼ full)
   bloodied napkin
   1 pair white stockings
Armand's pants/shirt — Pierre Iv (run by wardrobe after
   Iiii)
GARDEN CHAISE w/ 3 small pillows — IIii
Pair pants/shirt (to be packed) — Pierre IIi
Toiletries bag (to be packed) — Pierre IIi
6 Eggs (for basket) — Clemence IIii

ON STAGE:
PIANO — Black shawl draped on piano.
   Ashtray
   2 MORE cigarettes/matches — Sophie Ii
Cigar box (3 cigars/matches)
   Black fan — Marguerite Iiii
SCREEN U.L.
OPERA TABLE U.L. — 2 ashtrays glued down.
STAND w/ STATUE U.L.
IN SHOP:
Vase flowers (hand-off) — Pierre Iiii
Trunk (to be pre-set) — IIi
Bird stand — IIii
MAINTENANCE CLOSET:
Chaise w/ 6 pillows — Iii-Iiii
Ottoman (on top of chaise) — Iii-Iiii
DRESSING ROOMS:
LADIES'

ACT I —
Marguerite — Fan
Coin purse (to Sophie) — Ii
Sophie — Fan
Clemence — Fan
Prudence — Fan
Jorgnette
Reticule w/black book/pencil — Iii
Janine — Moonstone collar — Iii
   Pearls
   Brooch

ACT II —
Marguerite — Fan
Sophie — Parasol
   Fan

Clemence — Parasol
  Pearls
  Fan
  Bracelet (to Olympe) — IIiii
Prudence — Parasol
  Fan
Olympe — Fan
Yvette — Handkerchief
THE EMERALDS (in cup on wardrobe table)
MEN'S
Armand — Handkerchief — Iiii
Old Duke — Cane
  15 money notes in pocket — Iii
De Sancerre — Cane
  Billfold w/ 6 money notes
Druftheim — Coin purse w/ 8 gold coins — I
Armand — 5 money notes in pocket — IIiv
Father — Legal papers — IIi
  2 money notes — IIi
  2 gold coins — IIiii
Old Duke — Cane
Priest — Pouch w/ Holy water (w/ costume)
INTERMISSION:
STRIKE: BED to O.S.R.
2 SM.RND.TABLES — 1 O.S.L.
                  1 O.S.R.
ARMCHAIR to Maintenance Closet
DRESSING TABLE to D.L.VOM
Cover Chaise w/ sheet, add pillow board
CAMELLIAS on top of sheet
3 CHAIRS — D.R.VOM
2 CHAIRS — D.L.VOM
3 CHAIRS — IN SHOP
OTTOMAN — D.R.VOM

1 OPERA TABLE D.R.VOM
1 OPERA TABLE D.L.VOM
OVAL TABLE in office.

PRE-SET: TRUNK (open-tray on floor) IIi
   Pair boots/tan socks IIi

PROP PRE-SETS:

O.S.L.

1. 4 Large Pillows — Arm/Clem-IIii
Tray — 3 glasses champagne (½ full) — Dave IIiii
SM.RND.TABLE: IIiv-IIv
Candelabra/ashtray glued down on top.
2. Bird Cage w/ 2 doves — Marguerite IIii
1 Dustcover behind screen — Jay IIv

D.L.VOM

2 Dustcovers — Nick IIv

O.S.R.

SM.RND.TABLE: IIiv-IIv
Tray — Cognac decanter (½ full)
2 cognac glasses (¼ full)

D.R.VOM

Bottle champagne (¼ full) — Nick IIiii
Tray — 3 champagne glasses (½ full) — Nick IIiii
Chamber pot w/ blood (napkin covering) — Yvette IIiv
3 Dustcovers — David IIv
Blood Recipe
2 tspns. cornstarch
add a little water & mix well. Smooth out all lumps.
large spoonful peanut butter
approx. 2 oz corn syrup — mix well

add half of a bottle of a Karo light corn syrup
add 3 capfuls of red food coloring
approx. 11 drops blue
4 green
2 yellow

COSTUME PLOT

CLEMENCE

ACT I

Prologue & Scene 1
Corset & Petticoats
Pink Gown
Pink Pumps
Jewelry
Headpiece, Bag, Fan & White Gloves

Scene 3
Corset & Petticoats
Red Paisley Dress
Black Pumps
Jewelry
Headpiece, Bag, Black Gloves

ACT II

Scene 2
Corset & Petticoats
Yellow Dress
Satin Pumps
Jewelry
Bonnet, Bag & Parasol

Scenes 3,4,5
Same as ACT I — 1

MARGUERITE GAUTIER

ACT I

Scene 1
Wig #1 (Styled up)

Camisole, Bloomers, Corset & Petticoats
White Sequined Gown
Ivory Pumps
Jewelry, Flowers, Fan, & Bag

Scene 2
Camisole, Bloomers, Corset & Petticoats
Gold Gown
Silver Pumps
Jewelry

Scene 3
Same as above

Scene 4
Hair down
Silk Nightgown

Scene 5
Same as above
Add Ivory Silk Peignoir
Onstage add stockings

ACT II

Scene 2
Wig #2 (Styled up)
Camisole, Bloomers, Corset & Petticoats
Pink Print Dress
Pink Pumps
Jewelry

Scene 3
Camisole, Bloomers, Corset & Petticoats
Black Patterned Silk Chiffon Gown
Black Satin Pumps
Jewelry
Gloves & Flowers

Scene 4
Hair down
White Cotton Nightgown
Gold Cross
Onstage add White Cotton Peignoir

Scene 5
Ivory Silk Nightgown
Ivory Silk Peignoir

PRUDENCE

ACT I

Prologue & Scene 1
Corset & Petticoats
Gray Gown
Gray Pumps
Jewelry
Headpiece, Lorgnette, Fan, Bag & Gloves

Scene 2
Same as above, except Headpiece & Gloves & Bag
Add Blue & Grey Print Coat
Hat, Purse, Grey Gloves

Scene 3
Corset & Petticoats
Purple Paisley Dress
Black Pumps
Jewelry
Headpiece, Bag, & Black Lace Gloves

ACT II

Scene 2
Corset & Petticoats

Magenta Dress
Jewelry
Grey Tie Shoes
Bonnet, Bag, Parasol & Gloves

Scenes 3,4,5
Same as ACT I — 1

SOPHIE

ACT I

Prologue & Scene 1
Corset, Bloomers & Petticoats
Lavendar Gown
Grey Pumps
Jewelry
Headpiece, Fan & Gloves

Scene 2
Remove all of above except Undergarments

Scene 3
Corset & Petticoats
Striped Gown
Black Pumps
Jewelry
Headpiece & Gloves

ACT II

Scene 2
Corset & Petticoats
Rust Cotton Dress
Satin Pumps
Jewelry
Bonnet, Bag & Parasol

Scenes 3,4,5
Same as ACT I — 1
No Fan, Bag, Jewelry
Hat w/Veil
ACT II Jewelry

JANINE

ACT I

Scene 2
Corset, Bloomers & Petticoats
Black Striped Maids Dress
Black Boots
Maids Hat
Garter w/Bag

Scenes 3 & 5
Same as above

ACT II

Scene 3
Corset & Petticoats
Blue & Orange Gown
Satin Shoes
Jewelry
Headpiece & Gloves

YVETTE

ACT I

Scene 2
Corset & Petticoats
Brown Velveteen Dress

Black Boots
Apron
Grey Cap
Crocheted Shawl

ACT II

Scene 2
Same as ACT I

Scenes 4 & 5
Same as above except for Apron & Shawl
Add Black Chiffon Shawl

ARMAND DUVAL

ACT I

Prologue & Scene 1
White Shirt & Vest
Black Tail Suit
Cravat
Black Formal Pumps
Opera Cape & Top Hat

Scene 3
Same as above except change to Brocade Vest

Scene 4
Remove all of above except briefs

Scene 5
Same as above
Onstage add Black Formal Pants & Shirt

ACT II

Scenes 1 & 2
Striped Silk Shirt
Plaid Wool Vest
Leather Breeches
Black Boots
Onstage Scene 1 add Green Jacket

Scenes 3,4,5
Same as ACT I — 1

MARQUIS DE SAINT BRIEUC

ACT II

Scene 1
Black 3 pc. Suit
Black Boots
White Shirt
Black Cravat
Black Top Hat

Scene 2
Same as above except change to Red Cravat

ACT II

Scene 1
White Shirt
Black Cravat
Yellow Striped Vest
Tail Suit
Black Shoes

Scene 2
White Shirt
Brown Cravat
Brown & Green Vest
Grey Leather Breeches
Grey Tail Coat
Brown Boots

APPRAISER

ACT II

Scene 5
White Shirt
Brown 3 pc. Suit
Dark Brown Cravat
Black Shoes
Brown Top Hat

FOOTMEN

ACTS I & II
White Shirt & Tie
Tail Suit
Striped Vest
Black Shoes

PRIEST

ACT II

Scene 5
Black Cassock

White Surplus
Red Stole
Black Shoes

OLD DUKE

ACT I

Scene 1
White Shirt, Vest & Cravat
Tail Suit
Black Shoes
Opera Cape & Top Hat

Scene 2
Same Shirt
3 pc. Frock Suit
Brown Boots
Cravat
Inverness Cape & Brown Top Hat

ACT II

Scene 1
Same as ACT I — 1

DE SANCERRE

ACT I

Scenes 1 & 3
White Shirt, Vest & Cravat
Tail Suit
Black Shoes

Opera Cape & Top Hat

RUSSIAN PRINCE

ACT II

Scenes 3 & 4
Union Shirt
Uniform
Black Boots

COUNT DRUFTHEIM

ACT I

Scene 1
White Shirt, Vest & Cravat
Tail Suit
Black Shoes
Opera Cape & Top Hat

Scene 3
Same as above except change to Brocade Vest

ACT II

Scene 3
Same as ACT I — 1

JEAN-PAUL

ACT I

Scene 2
White Shirt

Brown Pants
Black Boots
Tweed Jacket

ACT II

Scene 2
Print Shirt
Striped Pants
Same Jacket & Boots

PIERRE

ACT I

Scene 2
White Shirt
Black Formal Pants
Yellow Striped Vest
Black Shoes
Apron

Scene 3
White Shirt
Tail Suit
Blue Brocade Vest
Black Shoes

Scene 5
Same as above

ABOUT THE PLAYWRIGHT

Pam Gems began writing for the theatre when she arrived in London in the early 1970s. Her early plays include BETTY'S WONDERFUL CHRISTMAS; AFTER BIRTHDAY, MY WARREN & THE AMIABLE COURTSHIP OF MIZ VENUS AND WILD BILL; GO WEST YOUNG WOMAN; and GUINEVERE, which were produced at Cockpit Theatre, Almost Free Theatre, the Roundhouse and Soho Poly between 1972 and 1976.

Her first commercial success was DUSA, FISH, STAS, AND VI, which was produced at the Edinburgh Festival, Hampstead Theatre Club and Mayfair Theatres in 1976 and 1977. The play explores the choices facing contemporary women whose generation has been affected by feminism and sexual liberation. Ms. Gems' work has focused on the reclaiming of women's history in such plays as QUEEN CHRISTINA, PIAF and now CAMILLE, all of which received their premieres at the Royal Shakespeare Company.

Her most recent plays are PASIONARIA, produced at the Newcastle Playhouse, and THE DANTON AFFAIR at the Barbican for the Royal Shakespeare Company, both of which explore a more overtly political sphere.

OTHER TITLES AVAILABLE FROM SAMUEL FRENCH

ANON
Kate Robin

Drama / 2m, 12f / Area

Anon. follows two couples as they cope with sexual addiction. Trip and Allison are young and healthy, but he's more interested in his abnormally large porn collection than in her. While they begin to work through both of their own sexual and relationship hang-ups, Trip's parents are stuck in the roles they've been carving out for years in their dysfunctional marriage. In between scenes with these four characters, 10 different women, members of a support group for those involved with individuals with sex addiction issues, tell their stories in monologues that are alternately funny and harrowing..

In addition to Anon., Robin's play What They Have was also commissioned by South Coast Repertory. Her plays have also been developed at Manhattan Theater Club, Playwrights Horizons, New York Theatre Workshop, The Eugene O'Neill Theater Center's National Playwrights Conference, JAW/West at Portland Center Stage and Ensemble Studio Theatre. Television and film credits include "Six Feet Under" (writer/supervising producer) and "Coming Soon." Robin received the 2003 Princess Grace Statuette for playwriting and is an alumna of New Dramatists.

SKIN DEEP
Jon Lonoff

Comedy / 2m, 2f / Interior Unit Set
In *Skin Deep*, a large, lovable, lonely-heart, named Maureen Mulligan, gives romance one last shot on a blind-date with sweet awkward Joseph Spinelli; she's learned to pepper her speech with jokes to hide insecurities about her weight and appearance, while he's almost dangerously forthright, saying everything that comes to his mind. They both know they're perfect for each other, and in time they come to admit it.

They were set up on the date by Maureen's sister Sheila and her husband Squire, who are having problems of their own: Sheila undergoes a non-stop series of cosmetic surgeries to hang onto the attractive and much-desired Squire, who may or may not have long ago held designs on Maureen, who introduced him to Sheila. With Maureen particularly vulnerable to both hurting and being hurt, the time is ripe for all these unspoken issues to bubble to the surface.

"Warm-hearted comedy … the laughter was literally show-stopping. A winning play, with enough good-humored laughs and sentiment to keep you smiling from beginning to end."
– *TalkinBroadway.com*

"It's a little Paddy Chayefsky, a lot Neil Simon and a quick-witted, intelligent voyage into the not-so-tranquil seas of middle-aged love and dating. The dialogue is crackling and hilarious; the plot simple but well-turned; the characters endearing and quirky; and lurking beneath the merriment is so much heartache that you'll stand up and cheer when the unlikely couple makes it to the inevitable final clinch."
– *NYTheatreWorld.Com*

OTHER TITLES AVAILABLE FROM SAMUEL FRENCH

BLUE YONDER
Kate Aspengren

Dramatic Comedy / Monolgues and scenes
12f (can be performed with as few as 4 with doubling) / Unit Set

A familiar adage states, "Men may work from sun to sun, but women's work is never done." In Blue Yonder, the audience meets twelve mesmerizing and eccentric women including a flight instructor, a firefighter, a stuntwoman, a woman who donates body parts, an employment counselor, a professional softball player, a surgical nurse professional baseball player, and a daredevil who plays with dynamite among others. Through the monologues, each woman examines her life's work and explores the career that she has found. Or that has found her.